SONYA E

REALM OF MIRRORS

ᚹᚾᛏᛗᚱ_ᛣᚫᚢᚱᛏ

THE DEATHSPEAKER CODEX: BOOK 3

Thank you for picking up *Realm of Mirrors.* Follow me on Amazon to be among the first notified about new releases in The DeathSpeaker Codex series.

- - - - - - - - - - - - - - - -

ISBN-13: 978-1532946868

ISBN-10: 1532946864

- - - - - - - - - - - - - - - -

More books by Sonya Bateman

WRONG SIDE OF HELL

The DeathSpeaker Codex, Book 1

FIELDS OF BLOOD

The DeathSpeaker Codex, Book 2

COMING SOON:

RETURN OF THE HUNTERS

The DeathSpeaker Codex, Book 4

Available from Amazon and wherever books are sold:

MASTER OF NONE | MASTER AND APPRENTICE

The Gavyn Donatti series – Available for Kindle and wherever books are sold

REALM OF MIRRORS

PROLOGUE

Winter Court, Arcadia – Thirty Years Ago

He cringed at the sound of her tread on the dungeon steps, and despised himself for it.

For a fortnight she'd kept him down here, stripped of his power—and everything else. His clothing, his dignity. The Court's sadistic *cáesdhe* had done their work well. If not for these chains, he'd no longer be on his feet.

But he would not yield.

She approached him slowly, and he could not help but tremble. Her beauty was undeniable, her power nearly boundless. Without his own magic, resisting her charms came at a painful price—and of course, she knew that.

It was a price he'd pay to keep his love safe.

"Oh, my. You seem so tired, *gallae*." The mere sound of her voice tore at him. "Wouldn't you like to rest?"

"Not in your bed," he gasped. "Highness."

A sweet, false smile. "In hers, then? You've only to tell me where she is, and I'll have her brought to you."

"Aye. In pieces." He managed a glare. "You'll not touch her."

"Where is she?"

Despite the promise of pain in those words, he said nothing.

"*Miilé lahn!*" She gestured fiercely at him. A hoarse cry escaped as a thousand phantom knives filled his body. "*Where is she?*"

He gasped again and spat blood. "Safe from you," he panted. When he'd sensed the Unseelie Guard, his own men, coming for him, his son had agreed to take her to the one place the Queen could not reach her—across the Veil, to the human realm. He'd also given the master stone to his lieutenant, Levoran, who'd promised to keep it from her hands and deliver it to his blood when the time came.

If she'd not managed to destroy every trace of his lineage by then.

She moved closer, until he could feel the passing of her breath on his skin. "A human," she murmured. "All this suffering, this humiliation...for a *human*. A disgusting, filthy insect." Her eyes searched his, and in them was nothing but the coldness of the ages. "At least tell me why," she said.

Drawing breath was difficult. "You'd not understand, Highness," he grated. "You do not love."

She backhanded him, hard enough to split his lip. "How dare you!" she roared. "I am the core of the storm, the blood of all hearts. The very essence of passion!"

"Aye, you've passion unmatched," he whispered...and thought, *but not love*. She loved no one save herself.

"And yet you refuse me." She grabbed his hair and forced his head up. "You'll bed Seelie and Unseelie, noble and lowborn, all manner of Arcadian peoples. And even a human. A human over me, your Queen."

"Highness...Moirehna, please." He knew she'd not see, but he had to try. "I've sworn to protect you with my life. This I have done, for centuries," he said. "But I cannot protect you from within the silk prison of your bed."

"You'll do as your Queen commands." She released him roughly. "You will tell me where she is, and you will serve me as I desire. Or I will destroy you."

He shuddered and straightened as best he could. "Kill me, then, because you'll never have her. Or me."

Her eyes flashed, and for a moment he was certain she would strike him dead. But then, she smiled. "Very well, *gallae*. You'll have your life, and your filthy little pet. In fact, you'll have all the humans you can desire," she said. "You will be brought before the Winter Court, and banished from Arcadia. But first...you will suffer."

As she spoke, four *cáesdhe* descended the steps.

No...three *cáesdhe*. And Levoran.

Though his face was as expressionless as the Court torturers, misery filled his lieutenant's eyes. Levoran would follow orders—and he was grateful for that, at least. Her threats to destroy him were empty, but she'd not hesitate to strike Levoran down.

She leaned toward him, her smile twisting on itself. "If you'd not sent your son to flee with the human whore, I'd have ordered him to do this. But your dear, trusted lieutenant will suffice."

The Queen moved back, but she did not leave the dungeon. She stayed to watch.

She watched until he no longer had the strength to scream.

CHAPTER 1

Manhattan, New York – Present Day

I still hadn't gotten used to the way people stared when we were out in public. Sadie and I could pass for normal, but Taeral—well, my brother kind of stood out. Even in Manhattan, land of the free and home of the weird. Nearly seven feet tall, with long black hair and a black duster over black clothes, and a silver metal arm longer than his normal one. The stares were worse in broad daylight.

At least Taeral didn't mind being stared at. He just hated the humans right back.

"You're certain this place is near," he said as we turned the corner at Seventh and Twenty-Ninth.

I nodded. "Abe said they have a file on it. Apparently, it's on the NYPD's watch list."

"For what?" Sadie said.

"Existing."

Eight years ago, The Grotto had been a run-of-the-mill, glass front tattoo shop sharing space with an occult bookstore on Forty-Second, between Ninth and Tenth. Now that space was a Starbucks. Four successive cab drivers and a search on Sadie's phone failed to turn up a new address, so I'd called Abe. Who'd been reluctant to give me a location for a vaguely suspicious tattoo studio that no one seemed to know anything about.

I couldn't blame him, really. I had my own suspicions, considering the owner of the shop in question had given me magic tattoos that I didn't know were magic until very recently. And then I found out the guy was some kind of rogue Seelie prince.

Being half Unseelie, I'd been forced to assume whatever magic they contained wasn't supposed to help me—since apparently the Seelie and Unseelie had a long tradition of trying to kill each other at every opportunity. Still, I'd had them eight years now, and the tattoos didn't seem to do much except glow.

Taeral was a lot more worried than me. And a lot more pissed—but he usually was. Angry was his baseline emotional state.

"All right," I said as we walked. "Tell me why we're doing this now, instead of taking a little time to recover from...oh, I don't know, fighting a pack of werewolves and a shitload of soldiers with super-weapons?"

We'd only been back in New York for a few days, after we'd helped Sadie save her family from Milus Dei—a whole new branch of the evil cult bastards we thought we'd already destroyed. Turned out there were pockets of them all over the world, with all sorts of fun plans to exterminate the Others. The one we'd just stopped involved a serum that temporarily gave humans the abilities of a werewolf, which would've let their soldiers kill just about anything.

I was still horrified at what I'd done to save the werewolves and humans they'd captured to experiment on, and I wasn't anywhere near ready to jump back into the supernatural fray. But here I was, making a surprise visit to a Seelie prince.

"I've explained this already," Taeral said. "It is the new moon. We cannot afford to wait another month—we must know what he's done to you."

"Right." I'd gotten that much, at least. Fae magic was tied to the moon. Every Fae had a spark, a certain capacity for magic, and once that was used up they needed moonlight to recharge. I had a slight advantage there because of the moonstone. The pendant I always wore, which had come to me under strange circumstances, was a kind of battery for storing moonlight that I could tap into when my spark ran low. "So you think this guy's going to try using magic against us," I said.

"Aye, I do." Taeral stared ahead without expression. "But in this realm at least, no Fae can kill another when the moon hides it face."

"Jesus, you think he'll try to *kill* us?"

Taeral shrugged. "He is, allegedly, a Seelie prince. We cannot risk believing he won't."

I didn't like the sound of that. Cobalt had seemed like such a nice guy when he gave me the tattoos. He'd done it all for free, over multiple sessions, once I'd gotten enough nerve to explain why I wanted them—to cover the scars.

The process had taken weeks. Because I had a lot of scars.

"Okay, let me get this straight," I said. "If there's no moon, then no one can kill us?"

"No *Fae* can." Taeral frowned slightly. "This restriction does not apply to humans."

"Oh." So much for being safe from Milus Dei for a few days a month.

Sadie, who'd pulled ahead of us a bit and crossed the next side street, stopped and waited at the curb. "You said the address is 542, right?" she said as we caught up.

"Yeah, why?"

"Because we already passed 540 back there. And this is 544."

I frowned, glanced at the building just ahead, and saw 544 on the window of the door. "What the hell?"

"There was no 542," she said.

I shook my head. "There has to be," I said, doubling back across the side street.

For some reason, the first building on the block was further away than it looked. Walking toward it made my head swim a little. But when I reached the door, the numbers above it read 540.

I turned to find Taeral and Sadie approaching, both with uneasy looks. "Maybe your captain friend gave you the wrong address," Sadie said. "I mean, there just isn't a 542 here."

"Actually, there is," Taeral said slowly. "The place is warded."

"It's what?"

"Warded. There are protection spells here...against the Unseelie," he said. "A kind of camouflage that prevents us from finding the entrance."

"Hold on. I'm not Unseelie," Sadie said. "So why can't I see it?"

"Because it is our proximity that triggers the spell." He put a hand on my arm. "Move back, Gideon," he said. "Sadie, stay where you are."

I frowned and started backing up. "How do we know when we're far enough away?"

"We'll know."

Sadie watched us warily. "Um, Taeral? Are these spells going to do something...weird to me?"

"No, *a'ghreal*," he said with a faint smile. "You are perfectly safe."

"All right." She didn't sound convinced.

We'd gotten two or three buildings away when Sadie started to shimmer.

I stopped to glare at Taeral. "You said it wouldn't do anything to her."

"It hasn't," he said. "What you are seeing is your perception, because the spell affects you. Not her. Now, move away."

"Fine." I shuffled back another few steps.

Sadie blurred, and then vanished.

Okat, that wasn't nothing. "Where the hell is she?" I said.

"Holy shit!"

11

Sadie's voice sounded like it was traveling through a tunnel, and it kind of creeped me out to hear it coming from the empty sidewalk in front of us. I could still see the cross street beyond, and the buildings on the other side. "Guys, there's a building here," she said. "It...wasn't here before. There's a door, but no address numbers on it."

"That is the place." Taeral started forward again.

I followed him and watched Sadie pop back into existence, staring open-mouthed at the exposed side of building 540. "It just stopped being there," she said as she turned to look at us. "And it wasn't like disappearing. I can't explain it. The building wasn't there, then it was, and then it...wasn't again."

"Great," I said. "So how do we get in?"

Taeral looked at the place where the building should've been, even though there wasn't enough room for another building. "I can break the wards," he said. "I'll not exhaust my spark doing it, but I will not be at full power. And obviously this Cobalt means us harm, if he's warded against the Unseelie."

"I'm not sure about that," I said. "Besides, we have to take the chance, right?"

"Right," Sadie said. "And if it comes down to it, I've got my luna-ball."

"Uh, let's try to avoid going wolf in the middle of Manhattan."

She snorted. "Do you really think I'd do it unless I had to?"

"Enough," Taeral said abruptly. "I'll handle the wards. And we'll all be prepared to do what is necessary."

I sighed. "Fine. Go for it."

Taeral faced the building that wasn't there, closed his eyes and held out his metal arm. He murmured something I could only hear enough to know the words were Fae—and pale blue light glowed from the runes etched into his hand and arm. The air in front of him shimmered, the way Sadie had when we backed away.

And then the building...was.

CHAPTER 2

"Okay. How in the hell did he hide a whole building?"

I couldn't stop staring. The two-story brick structure that wasn't there a minute ago was nothing like The Grotto I'd been to. The only windows were on the second floor, and the door was a solid, dull green metal with a push bar instead of a knob. There were no words or numbers anywhere on the place, and nothing to indicate this was a tattoo shop.

No wonder the NYPD was suspicious. This place had shady written all over it—I half expected some bouncer with biceps the size of my head to step out and demand the secret password.

"He'd not hidden it from everyone. Just the Unseelie," Taeral said. "That requires less power than a complete warding. But still, it is no simple spell."

"So I guess he's pretty powerful."

"Aye. If the rumors are true."

"Well, let's find out," Sadie said as she walked up to the door and pushed the bar. Nothing happened. "Er. It's locked," she said.

"Then I'll unlock it." Taeral moved for the entrance.

"Whoa, hold it," I said. "Maybe they're not open right now."

He stared at me. "And?"

"Look, it's one thing to take apart a bunch of spells. But if we just unlock the door and walk in, we're breaking and entering."

"So?"

I sighed. "One of those things is just a really bad idea. The other one is illegal. Besides, if the place is closed, that means no one's here anyway." I stepped up next to Sadie. "Let's try this first, okay?" I said, and knocked on the door.

Nothing happened. After a minute or so, I knocked harder.

"This is pointless," Taeral snapped. "Let me—"

"Wait. I hear something in there," Sadie said. "Footsteps."

"I don't hear anything," I said.

She rolled her eyes. "Werewolf. Enhanced senses. Remember?"

"Oh, right."

Then I did hear something faint, like footsteps. There was a pause, a click, and the door opened a few inches. One bleary brown eye peered out. "Sorry. We're not buying, and we don't need Jesus, thanks," a male voice said, just before the door started closing.

The voice sounded a little familiar, but I couldn't place it.

"Hold on," I said quickly. "I'm looking for Cobalt, and I'm not selling anything. Including Jesus."

The door paused and the gap widened slowly, revealing a man with light brown hair, a whisper of stubble and a puzzled frown, with a coffee mug clutched in his free hand. So much for familiar. I'd never seen him before, and he definitely wasn't Cobalt—who was tall, dark-haired, and had quite a few tattoos and piercings. I wasn't that great at sensing Others yet, but this guy seemed human. "Do you have an appointment with him?" the man said.

"Uh, no. But he did some work for me, and I had a few questions about it."

"Well, he doesn't open until four. He's here, but I don't know…" The man leaned aside to look at Sadie, and then Taeral. His expression grew guarded, and he glanced at something off to the side. Then he frowned. "You're not welcome in this house."

15

"Huh?"

Before I could react any further, something pushed against me. For a second I thought it was the brown-haired man, but he hadn't moved.

Then my feet actually slid back on the sidewalk about half an inch. And I couldn't go forward at all.

It took me a few seconds to figure it out. There was some kind of magic law that said no Fae could enter the property of another Fae if they weren't wanted. We'd had this problem with Reun, the Seelie noble who was now staying with us at the Castle—another long story. Taeral hadn't exactly been open to his presence at first, with good reason, so he told him he wasn't welcome. And Reun physically couldn't come back into the place until Taeral invited him.

"How—you are not Fae," Taeral said.

"No, but you are." The man stared evenly at him. "And this is my house as much as Cobalt's, so the Law still holds."

"You know of the Laws?"

"All right. That's it." Sadie bumped me in passing and brushed right past the man into the place, almost spilling his coffee. "Thing is, I'm not Fae," she said. "And you need to invite my friends inside, because they have to talk to Cobalt. Right now."

The man blinked rapidly and stared at her. "Um. You're trespassing?" he said. "Look, for humans I just call the cops."

She gave him the sweet smile I knew well—the one that said she was about to go off in the exact opposite way that smile suggested. "I'm not human, either."

"Okay. Everybody just...stop." I held back a groan. Sadie probably wouldn't go wolf just to prove a point—but probably was not the same as definitely. And any minute now, Taeral was going to start being his normal, threatening self. "Look," I said to the guy in the doorway. "You know about the Fae, so I guess I can explain this to you. Cobalt—"

"You know nothing about this human," Taeral snarled. "Do not trust him."

I closed my eyes briefly. I could almost read his mind—he was worried because the Fae couldn't kill each other without moonlight, but humans could. Any human with knowledge of the Fae might be a threat. But I didn't sense anything dangerous from this guy, and I wanted to give him the benefit of the doubt. Something Taeral couldn't do. "Trust *me*, all right?" I said to him. "Just give me a minute."

Taeral relented. A little.

I would've been upset with him, but there was another reason he was like this. Fae had to keep their promises, or they'd die—and he'd promised to protect me. Letting me get hurt could literally kill him. So, I'd just have to hope I could reason with this guy...or Taeral would. Only he'd use not so much 'reasoning' as 'violent persuasion.'

"Anyway," I said. "Cobalt did some tattoos for me, a long time ago. And I just found out they're not exactly normal tattoos. Know what I mean?"

"Uh...no," the man said.

I let out a frustrated breath. "They're magic. But I didn't ask for magic tattoos, and I have no idea what they are or what they do."

He looked almost startled. "Are you sure? I mean, that really doesn't sound like something Cobalt would do," he said. "Maybe you've got the wrong guy."

"Oh, aye," Taeral said. "Surely we're seeking some other bastard Seelie prince who owns a tattoo shop and calls himself Cobalt."

I just about choked trying not to laugh.

After a long pause, the man said, "All right. I guess maybe you'd better talk to him."

"Good idea," Sadie said.

"My name's Will, by the way," he said, moving back from the door. "And you are?"

"Gideon. That's Sadie, and Taeral," I said.

17

"Well, I'm not sure how nice it is to meet you yet. I'll let you know once I finish my coffee. We're night people around here." He flashed a half-smile. "Come in, Gideon. Taeral."

The vague pressure I'd almost stopped noticing vanished, and we walked inside.

CHAPTER 3

Beyond the entrance was a small, windowless room with two doors on the opposite side. There was a plain wooden table and chair off to the right, and what looked like a ledger book on the surface of the table.

And on the wall next to the entrance, glowing runes.

"It's kind of an alarm system," Will said when he noticed me looking at the symbols. "They glow when there's an, er..."

"Unseelie." Taeral probably could've sounded more disgusted, but he'd really have to work at it. "Not surprising, considering the wards on this place—and what your master is."

Will made a shocked, half-strangled sound that might've had a laugh in it somewhere. "Master?" he said. "Oh man, do you have the wrong idea. Cobalt is my partner."

"So you work here, too?" I said.

He smiled. The full expression this time. "Not that kind of partner. The shop's downstairs, and we live upstairs."

"Oh," I said. Then my brain caught up with the words. "Oh, *partner*," I said.

"Yes. Soon to be husband."

"Congratulations." Well, at least that explained why he knew about the Fae. They were together in a more-than-friends way. Cobalt would've had to tell him the truth.

The truth. All at once, I realized why his voice seemed familiar. I'd heard it in the life before the Others happened, when I was just a body mover trying to avoid involvement with the rest of the world. But I'd never heard it in person. "I know you," I said. "Well, I don't know you, but—you're Will Ambrose, right? You have that nighttime radio show. The Truth Will Out."

Will blushed a little. "Yeah, that's me," he said. "You're a listener?"

"Off and on. Well, I was until recently. Not that I don't like the show," I said. The Truth was a talk show, mostly dealing with LGBT relationships. From what I'd heard, this guy had helped a lot of people get through some serious shit. "I listened while I was driving around nights, for my job. But I'm semi-retired now."

"Oh. Cool." At least he seemed a little warmer now. "Well, I guess we should go talk to Cobalt," he said. "I have to warn you, though, he just woke up. He might be a little cranky."

"That's fine," I said, shooting a warning glance at Taeral. "We're the ones who just crashed your place. Hell, I'd be cranky too."

"All right. This way."

Will opened the door on the left, and we followed him up a flight of stairs. At the top was a kind of railed balcony with a step-down into a large, open loft room. Most of it was a living room, but along one side was a kitchenette and small dining nook. And on the other was a big picture window, with an incredible view of Manhattan that included the East River, sparkling in the early sun.

For the location alone, this place must've cost a fortune.

"So, uh, stay there a minute," Will said as he moved down the few steps to the loft. "I'll go get him."

He hadn't gotten ten steps when a door across the room opened, and Cobalt came out.

I had no problem recognizing him, but he was kind of scarier than I remembered. All he had on was a pair of shorts, and he looked ripped enough to bench press a car. Long, shaggy dark hair didn't quite conceal the tribal tattoos along the sides of his neck that spilled across his chest and shoulders. He had a silver ball stud just below his lower lip, a single hoop earring in one ear, and a bristling row of hardware along the edge of the other. Not exactly what I pictured when I thought fairy prince.

And he was way beyond a little cranky. Something close to fury simmered in his blue eyes—which were riveted on Taeral.

Will gave a nervous cough and hurried toward him. "Heh. Morning," he said.

"Yes, it is." Cobalt's gaze narrowed on us. "Friends of yours, love?"

"Not exactly. But, um..." He reached the bigger man, glanced back, and then stood on tiptoe to murmur something near Cobalt's ear.

The Seelie's expression changed from suspicion, to vague recognition, to something like resignation. "Gideon Black," he finally said. "It's been a long time."

Will's brow furrowed. "You know them?"

"Not them. Only him." Cobalt made a weary gesture in my general direction. "Come in, please," he said. "You'll have to excuse me if I grab some coffee before we chat. This is early for me."

I was surprised he remembered me. But before I could head for the couches, Taeral stopped me and whispered harshly, "I do not trust him. He's all but admitted he's done something to you."

"Maybe. But it looks like he feels bad about it," I whispered back. "I think we should give him a chance to explain."

"He is Seelie."

"Yeah, I've heard that," I said. "And you don't like it when people make assumptions about you because you're Unseelie. Right?"

"Right," Sadie said, circling behind me to thread her arm through Taeral's. "Come on, grumpy. The man asked us in. Let's go."

I tried not to be jealous of the way she looked at him, or the way he actually responded to her. They had a...thing. It wasn't exactly a relationship, but I knew they'd been very familiar with each other at least once or twice. And they still spent a lot of time alone together. Usually in his room, sometimes overnight.

It sucked having a crush on my brother's not-really-girlfriend.

Sadie, Taeral and I sat on the long couch facing the back of the room. There was a coffee table in front of it, and a matching loveseat on the other side where Cobalt took a seat next to Will, holding a steaming mug in both hands. "So," he said. "Should I assume you've noticed something strange about your tattoos?"

I nodded. "You could say that."

"I shouldn't have..." He sighed and sipped his coffee. "You'd no idea what you were, at the time," he said. "That much was obvious."

"So you thought to take advantage of his ignorance by casting enchantments on him?" Taeral said.

Cobalt frowned at him. "I'm sorry. Who are you?"

"His name's Taeral," I said quickly, before he could introduce himself in a less friendly way. "He's my brother."

"Your brother. Well, that explains a few things, at least."

"Really." Taeral's voice was dangerously calm. "What, exactly, does it explain?"

"Why you're so protective of him, and why you've assumed the worst of me."

His lip curled. "I've merely assumed that you are Seelie royalty. That alone is sufficient cause for mistrust, to say the least."

"Look, I'm not exactly—"

A tremendous bang sounded from below, making the floor shake a little. It was immediately followed by another slam, and then footsteps slapping the stairs.

Cobalt heaved a breath. "Speaking of protective older brothers," he murmured. "Here comes mine."

CHAPTER 4

Cobalt might've looked more threatening than I remembered, but I still didn't believe he'd hurt anyone.

His brother, on the other hand, scared the hell out of me.

The tall figure who charged up the stairs and strode across the room wore all black, like Taeral—but his outfit was leather and straps and hardware. He had collar-length, dark red hair, fierce green eyes, and a wicked-looking scar along his jaw. I had no doubt he was Fae, because I could feel the power radiating from him. Almost like he wanted to broadcast that he was not to be fucked with.

Taeral was already on his feet and facing the oncoming big brother. Before anyone else could react, he threw a hand out and shouted, "*Céa biahn!*"

The leather-clad Fae flew back and crashed into the balcony railing.

Then the whole room exploded in motion.

Cobalt bolted from the couch, headed for Taeral. Will lunged, trying to stop him, and missed. The brother bounded up almost instantly and drew an arm back, probably to throw a spell—and Sadie shot to her feet, going for the luna-ball in her pouch.

I stood slowly, aware that the moonstone had started glowing white fire. The way it did sometimes when I was feeling threatened. "Enough!"

Everyone stared at me.

"All right," I said, pinching the bridge of my nose. "Taeral is sorry for throwing you across the room...er, whoever you are. Cobalt's brother."

"Uriskel," Taeral said through clenched teeth. "And I am not sorry."

"Oh, good. Guess we don't have to introduce you two," I said.

"He is a traitor! The sadistic pet of the Seelie nobles," Taeral spat.

Cobalt's eyes took on a warning light. "Watch what you say about my brother," he said tightly.

"Your *brother*. What a bold lie, and no less than I'd expect from Seelie royalty." Taeral's hot glare moved to Uriskel. "He is Unseelie. And he's betrayed countless numbers of his own kind. Given them over to the Summer Court for torture, imprisonment. And execution."

Okay, that didn't sound good. I guessed I was right to be afraid of him.

Incredibly, Uriskel smiled. There wasn't anything close to happiness in that expression. "Guilty as charged," he said, executing a mocking bow. "Have I wronged someone you know, then? Taeral?"

"Aye. You have."

"Uriskel, please," Cobalt said hoarsely. "Don't let them think—"

"Cobalt." He infused the name with warning, and then stared coldly at Taeral. "Believe what you will about me," he said. "I'll not explain myself to the likes of you. But make no mistake—Cobalt *is* my brother, and I'll allow no harm to come to him."

"Likewise," Taeral snarled, moving closer to me.

"Ah, yes." Uriskel's green eyes settled on me in flat assessment. "You are the interesting one here, aren't you? You and your...moonstone," he said. "Though your werewolf friend makes a close second."

"What?" Will stammered, cutting a glance at Sadie. "Did he say werewolf?"

She shrugged. "It's true. I am."

"Holy..."

"Yeah. That's about what I thought when I found out," I said, relieved that things had calmed down a little. Even the moonstone had settled to a dull shine. But the relief might not last long, since everyone except me and Will seemed ready to attack at the slightest provocation. "Listen, can we all agree not to kill each other? We didn't come here to cause trouble."

"Then why *did* you come here?" Uriskel said. "And who's broken my wards?"

"Is that what's summoned you, brother?" Cobalt flashed a wry smile. "Well, I'm afraid they're here because I made a mistake. One I was about to explain before your...ah, dramatic entrance."

Uriskel sighed. "Very well," he said. "I suppose I'll not harm anyone. Yet."

When no one else chimed in, I gave a deliberate cough. "Taeral?"

"Fine," he grunted. "I will refrain from attacking the traitor. For the moment."

"Trust me, I'd rather not hurt anyone," Sadie said. "I didn't bring any extra clothes."

Will blinked at her, and then gave me a strange look.

"You don't want to know," I said.

"And I'll not harm anyone, even if they insult my brother. Though I'd appreciate it if they'd not speak of things they don't understand." Cobalt's shoulders slumped, and he shook his head once. "Can we try this again?" he said. "Please, sit down."

It was times like this I really wished life had a reset button, because I couldn't see this conversation going well.

Grudging introductions were made. Uriskel refused to join us, instead choosing to stand next to the big window with his arms folded and his back against the wall, glaring at everyone.

I still didn't know what to make of him. There was no doubt he'd done the things Taeral said. He didn't even try to deny it. But he obviously loved his brother, and Cobalt seemed almost pained by the subject. Like there was a good reason his brother was a bastard, even though Uriskel refused to share.

And I had to admit, the whole brother thing did seem suspicious. I didn't know a lot about the Fae, but it did seem pretty much impossible. The Seelie and Unseelie were different species, I thought—so this was like trying to believe a goldfish and a pit bull were brothers.

I definitely didn't see the resemblance. But I also couldn't completely brush it off, because my brother was a...Taeral.

Cobalt picked up his coffee mug from the table, and then put it back down. "First, let me explain this," he said. "I'm no prince."

"That's not what I've heard," Taeral said.

"Yes, I know the rumors." He frowned slightly. "By birth only, I am the son of the former Seelie King. But I've never known the bastard, and I'm glad for that."

Taeral raised an eyebrow. "Former?"

"Aye, the Summer Court has a new king now," he said. "It happened very recently, and it's a story for another time. But I was banished from Arcadia years ago, long before I knew about my...royal blood."

Something in Taeral's posture relaxed, and I was glad for it. He knew a little something about being banished. Not him personally, but his father. Our father, technically speaking. I didn't know much of the story, but the Unseelie Queen had banished Daoin, and Taeral chose to stay in the human realm with him out of loyalty.

It was a choice that hadn't turned out well for either of them.

"So about your tattoos," Cobalt said. "I assure you, they're not intended for harm. And I believed you'd never realize they were enchanted, because…well, you clearly did not know you were Fae. I assumed you were a changeling."

"I was, actually," I said, surprised he'd figured that out. "And I'm only half Fae."

Uriskel made a derisive sound. "That explains *your* brother, at least," he said.

"Don't." Cobalt shot a firm look at him. "Anyway," he said to me. "Most changelings never know what they are. You must know what it takes for one to realize their potential, since you're aware of your true self."

"Yeah. I had a little help with that." Taeral had to explain the changeling thing to me, when I still didn't trust a word he said—and I'd had to dig up the remains of my real mother, a woman I'd never met and didn't know existed, since she died giving birth to me.

Then I had a conversation with her.

I decided it wasn't a great idea to tell these people I'd just met that I was the DeathSpeaker. Most of the Others seemed to know what that meant, and it wasn't usually welcome news.

After all, Milus Dei wanted to use me as a genocide weapon to wipe them all out.

"I can imagine who might've helped you." Cobalt smiled slightly.

"You're probably right," I said. "So what do the tattoos do? I mean, besides glow. And why did they start glowing?"

He looked around uneasily. "I'm not sure whether you want me to discuss certain…aspects of your circumstances in front of others."

At first I had no idea what he meant. Then I remembered how awkward it was when I went to him the first time. There I'd been, eighteen and stupid, trying to stumble through some total bullshit story about why I'd wanted cover-ups without actually saying the word *scars*.

I think at one point, I even asked him if I could get tattoos without taking off my shirt.

27

"You mean the scars," I finally said. "Yeah, it's fine. Discuss away."

"All right." He glanced at Will, and I wondered why. But he didn't elaborate. "Well, I'd never seen a Fae so marked," he said. "We don't scar easily. If you're half human, that accounts for some of it, but..." Suddenly, he couldn't look at me. "You seemed lost. Defenseless. And I wanted to help."

"Uh-huh." I couldn't help noticing he still hadn't gotten to the point. "So, how did you?"

He made a vague gesture. "For the most part, the enchantments help to guide you along the Path."

"Um, great. What's that?"

"It is a Fae's sense of place, of being," Taeral said before Cobalt could answer, looking at him with something other than fury for once. "And a heightened awareness of danger."

Cobalt nodded. "Quite useful in a city like this. Since you didn't seem to have access to your abilities, I sought to give you something that would've felt natural, even if you'd not known why."

"Oh. Well, thanks. I think." That didn't sound bad. But he'd also said 'for the most part,' which meant there was more. "And what else do they do?" I said. "There's still the glowing thing."

"I did not expect them to glow," Cobalt said softly. "You were so damaged, and I'd no idea whether...whatever caused that damage was still a threat. So I cast an enchantment that would boost your healing and hold back those who intended you harm, in the event you were critically injured. Your natural healing must have made the magic visible."

Right then I understood why he was so reluctant to explain this. It wasn't a bad thing either. He just knew I must've been critically injured recently, because it was the only way I would've noticed the tattoos did anything.

At the time I realized it, I'd been half-dead on the ground, surrounded by Milus Dei soldiers who had weapons and wanted to make me all dead. But they'd backed away, because they were afraid.

I had no idea why. Until now.

"Good news," I said. "They work."

Cobalt gave a sad smile. "Yes, I gathered that. I'm only sorry you had to learn this firsthand."

"All right. This is all very touching," Uriskel drawled as he straightened and strode toward the couches. "And now that you've had your explanation, you'll get out of my brother's house."

CHAPTER 5

It was a real effort not to get up and walk out of the place right then, before Uriskel could do something unpleasant to make us.

Cobalt rose to meet his brother. "You're right. It is my house," he said quietly. "That means I decide who stays, and who goes."

"Really, Cobalt. Your soft heart will be your downfall yet." Uriskel bared his teeth at Taeral. "That one is dangerous," he said. "And the female is a *werewolf.* You do realize what that means?"

Sadie was on her feet before either of us could stop her. "*I* don't know what it means," she said. "Why don't you tell me?"

"Your kind is a threat to us."

"You don't know me!"

"Aye. And none of you know me. Nor will you, ever." Uriskel's hands clenched into white-knuckled fists as he faced Cobalt again. "If you'll not make them leave, brother, then I'll take mine. Be it on your head if anything happens."

I thought I saw hurt in his eyes as he turned and stalked away. But I was probably imagining that. I doubted much of anything could hurt him.

Cobalt watched him go, and let out a sigh. "I must speak with him," he said. "And I hope you realize that he's right. I should ask you to leave, if only because of the way you've treated him."

"He admits freely to what he is," Taeral said. "Why should he take offense at the truth?"

Cobalt's jaw clenched. "Just because he's used to being an object of contempt, does not mean he enjoys it," he said. "Excuse me."

No one moved until he started down the stairs. Then Sadie reclaimed her seat next to Taeral, and said, "Maybe you were a little hard on him."

"Really. And he was so pleasant to you," he said. "He is a murderous, scheming traitor. I'll not discuss this matter further."

"Fine. Don't."

The temperature in the room took a sudden plunge, metaphorically speaking. I suspected everyone would be sleeping in their own beds tonight.

After an awkward silence, Will cleared his throat. "So," he said. "You're a werewolf, huh?"

"Yep," Sadie said.

"What's that like?"

She smirked. "Overrated."

Just then, a raised voice drifted up the stairs. I couldn't make out the words, but it was Uriskel—and he was really, really pissed. The shouting cut off, and Cobalt murmured something in return. Then there was more shouting.

"Don't worry. They fight all the time. Brother stuff," Will said. But he looked distinctly uncomfortable, and I had the feeling this wasn't one of their usual fights. "Hey, I'm sorry about your scars," he said to me. "It's not easy having people talk about that stuff."

I shrugged and looked away. "It's fine."

"Sure it is." He stared at me until I looked back. "I was in an abusive relationship when I met Cobalt," he said. "It left scars. And it was a long time before I could talk about them, or tolerate anyone asking about them."

So that was why Cobalt looked to him before he started talking about my 'circumstances.' I felt bad for him, but sympathy didn't change anything. I knew that better than

31

most. "They're old scars. Ancient history," I murmured. "No big deal."

Of course, I was lying my ass off. They were a big deal, to me, and I still couldn't talk about them. But my ex-family was no one's business, especially someone I'd just met. I hadn't even told Sadie about my past. Taeral knew only the bare minimum—the Valentines had hated me, and enjoyed proving their hatred in creatively violent ways.

Another floor-rattling slam from below saved me from having to continue the conversation. It wasn't long before Cobalt reappeared, looking more than a little drained. "Well, at least you've no need to fear for your lives," he said. "Uriskel swears he'll no longer protect me, and will leave me to suffer the consequences of my own bad decisions."

Great. I hadn't actually been fearing for my life, until he said that.

Cobalt looked at Will. "Is there more coffee, love?" he said. "Maybe I could manage to drink some this time. And perhaps our guests would care for a cup?"

Taeral stood abruptly. "No need. We'll take our leave, as well." His rigid posture suggested he was about to say something stupid—again—but then he relaxed with a slight frown. "Thank you for the explanation, and for protecting my brother when I could not," he said stiffly. "And I apologize for insulting your…Uriskel."

With that, he pivoted and headed for the stairs.

"Um. I'd better go with him." Sadie got up and offered a tentative smile. "Nice to meet you guys," she said. "Gideon, we'll meet you outside? I'll just make sure he doesn't do anything he shouldn't."

I nodded. "Thanks, Sadie."

When she was out of sight, I faced Cobalt and made a helpless gesture. "Big brothers, right?" I said.

"Exactly. Sometimes, there are no words for them."

"Tell me about it." I smirked and held a hand out. "Good to see you again. And I do mean that."

"Likewise." Cobalt shook, but his expression pulled into a vague frown. "I couldn't help but notice that your brother is…troubled," he said. "In fact, there seems to be something hanging over all of you. Some dark cloud."

"Yeah. There's something, all right," I said. Wasn't going to get into the Milus Dei issue, or the more immediate problems we had with Daoin, and my being the DeathSpeaker. Taeral had plans to deal with those immediate problems—but it wasn't going to be easy. "We're figuring it out," I said. "It's a process."

"I imagine it is." Cobalt cocked his head slightly. "There are few resources available to the Fae in this realm," he said. "But should you need help, I may be able to provide it. It's something of a habit of mine, helping other Fae who've been banished or otherwise aren't welcome in Arcadia. A habit my brother tends to disagree with," he added with a crooked smile.

"Thanks," I said, thinking I'd probably never take him up on it. Mostly because Taeral would kill me.

I shook hands with Will. "Nice to put a face with the voice," I said.

"Always glad to meet a listener." He smiled. "Also, what Cobalt said. I'll help too, if I can. Even if you just need to talk sometime."

"Appreciate the offer," I said. "And I'd better get out there, because Mr. Cranky doesn't always listen to Sadie. Or, you know…anyone."

Cobalt grinned. "Somehow, that does not surprise me."

We said goodbye, and I headed out of The Grotto convinced it'd be the last time I set foot in the place. It was kind of a shame, because I liked Cobalt and Will. And we could always use more resources. Or preferably, more friends.

But there wasn't a chance in hell Taeral would put up with that.

CHAPTER 6

I figured when we got back to the Castle, Taeral would lecture me about keeping my mouth shut when I didn't know anything, and probably rant about Uriskel a while for good measure. But apparently he was serious when he said he wouldn't discuss it further.

He did ask Sadie and me to wait in the parlor while he got Daoin. So he definitely wanted to talk about something—only not what just happened.

The Castle was an abandoned hotel we'd kind of appropriated when we needed a home for a bunch of displaced Others. For the most part, we'd managed to clean the place up, restore electricity and running water, and furnish some of the common areas. Everyone had their own room and brought whatever they wanted into it. The Duchenes, our resident voodoo clan, had the whole top floor to themselves.

Once they'd claimed rooms, no one else wanted to share the space.

The old-fashioned parlor off the back of the hotel's lobby had been remodeled into something that was part sitting room, part home theater. The front half contained a few tables and chairs, some bookshelves, and an old bar counter where Taeral stashed the occasional bottle of booze he was trying not to drink. At the back was a big-screen TV and DVD player, a mismatched collection of couches and chairs, and a few growing stacks of movies that everyone contributed to.

Electricity we could get. Cable, not so much.

It was still before noon, so we had the room to ourselves. Most of the residents at the Castle were night people. Including me—and this was far too early for so much drama. Sadie sat at the table next to the window, and I took the chair across from her. "Did he say anything to you about all that?" I said.

"Not a thing. He's never mentioned Uriskel before."

"Yeah, well, he never talked about Reun either." The Seelie noble who'd helped Milus Dei destroy the Others' previous home had shown up here about a month ago, begging for the privilege of serving Daoin. Before then, Taeral would only say that Reun was dangerous. We finally got the whole story when he came here—that he'd done some horrible things to Taeral and a lot of other Unseelie back in Arcadia, and that Daoin should've been his mortal enemy because he'd slept with Reun's wife.

Reun had somehow accidentally killed her for that, but not before she'd erased all of his memories that included her. So Reun convinced himself that Daoin was the key to restoring the good things about his three hundred-odd years of marriage.

Unfortunately, Daoin had lost an entire lifetime of memories. Now Reun was practically glued to him, insisting that he had to protect him, and Taeral grudgingly tolerated his presence.

Sadie frowned, tracing aimless circles on the table with a finger. "He doesn't talk about Arcadia at all," she said. "Not for as long as I've known him. I'm really worried about this plan of his."

"That makes two of us."

I'd only known I was the DeathSpeaker for a couple of months, and the job hadn't come with an instruction manual. When it came to my abilities, I was basically winging it—and there were a few major problems. One, talking to the dead was painful. Especially if they didn't want to chat. The dead couldn't lie, and most of the corpses I'd spoken to hadn't wanted to part with the truth. The harder they resisted, the more it hurt. And two, I couldn't do it for long. I'd start to bleed from various orifices, and if I didn't break it off, I'd pass out.

But apparently, I wasn't the first DeathSpeaker. There'd been others before me—long dead now, but Taeral said there were some Fae still living who'd known the previous DeathSpeaker and might be able to help me figure all this out.

Unfortunately, they were in Arcadia. We'd have to go there to find them. And he wanted to take Daoin over too, in the hopes his father would regain the memories that Milus Dei had tortured out of him over twenty-six years of captivity. Reun had been able to help a little—enough that Daoin managed to remember he had two sons, most of the time. Not that he'd known me before.

The big problem was that Daoin had been banished. And for a banished Fae, returning to Arcadia was a death sentence.

It wasn't long before Taeral returned with Daoin. I'd gotten used to his appearance, but it was still a brief shock at first, every time. Daoin had forgotten that he had magic, so he didn't wear a glamour—a basic spell most Fae generated constantly to give them a human appearance. He was always in his true form. Blue skin, pointed ears, long limbs, and extra joints in his fingers. Twin crescent scars curved down either side of his face, markings Taeral had mentioned he'd had as long as he could remember.

The only thing not natural was his hair, which had gone white with shock shortly after we rescued him.

Daoin smiled as he entered the room. "Is it time for the movie?" he said.

"No, Father. Not yet." Taeral winced a little. I'd only known Daoin the way he was now—mostly cheerful, perpetually confused, and prone to spells of half-remembered horrors that could shut him down for hours, or days. But to Taeral, he was a once-proud warrior who'd been reduced to an empty shell, and it hurt him to see his father like this. "We'll watch the movie later tonight," he said.

"Yes. We're going to see The Godfather, aren't we?"

"We are."

"Oh, good." Daoin turned his attention to the table. "Hello, Gideon. Hello, Sadie," he said. "I've remembered your names, haven't I?"

"Yep, you got it," I said. "Right on the first try."

"If I say the names, I can remember. And you are...my son. Like Taeral."

"That's right."

Sometimes I almost understood how Taeral felt, even though I'd never gotten the chance to know the real Daoin. Now was one of those times.

"Father, we need to discuss something important," Taeral said as he guided him toward the table. "Do you feel up to having a conversation that may be...somewhat difficult?"

"Difficult?" Daoin gave a vague frown. "You mean because I forget things sometimes."

"Yes, because of that. But I'd like to talk about something that may help you remember."

Daoin glanced at him again, and then sat in one of the chairs. "Sure. I'd like to remember things," he said. "The way I remember that you're my son, and I'm your father. And my name is Daoin."

Taeral closed his eyes. "Aye," he said hoarsely. "Your name is Daoin."

I assumed he wanted to talk about going to Arcadia. As he took a seat between Daoin and Sadie, I said, "Are you sure this is a good idea?"

"No. I am certain of nothing." He raised a faint smile. "But I must try. And...I'd not wanted to have this conversation alone."

Okay, that was unexpected. Taeral never asked for help with anything. He wasn't exactly asking for it now, either, but he was more or less implying that he needed moral support. Which definitely wasn't like him.

Running into someone from the past must've shaken him a lot harder than he'd let on.

Taeral drew a deep breath and let it out slowly. "I'd like to take you on a journey," he said to Daoin. "To a place you've known before, a place you've forgotten. You and I, we come from this place. It was...home."

Daoin cocked his head slightly. "Is it a nice place?"

"It can be," Taeral said. "But there are dangers as well. The journey may be a great risk for you, Father. However, it may also be the only way to restore your memories, and return you to yourself."

"Does this place have a name?"

"Aye." Taeral hesitated, and finally said, "It is called Arcadia."

"Arcadia." The lingering smile melted from Daoin's lips. "She won't like that," he whispered, his eyes widening. "No, she won't like that at all. She means to..."

"Do you remember something?" Taeral said. "Someone from Arcadia? Do you know who she is?"

A visible shudder moved through him. "She does not love," he rasped.

Then he shot to his feet and stumbled back from the table. "You'll never have her!" he shouted, in a resonating voice like nothing I'd ever heard from him. His blue eyes nearly glowed with rage. "She is safe. The stone is safe. You'll not...have..."

"Father, no!" Taeral lunged at him as he swayed in place, catching him with an arm around his waist. "She is not here," he said. "This is your castle. Remember? Everyone is safe here. Everyone belongs."

"My castle." Confusion washed over his features. "Yes. I have a castle," he said with a smile. "We should go there. It has plenty of room."

Taeral pressed his lips together. "We are already in your castle, Father," he said.

"We are?" He looked around briefly and brightened. "Oh, yes. Is it time for the movie?"

The pained expression on Taeral's face was hard to take. "No," he whispered. "Not yet."

"Okay. We can watch the movie tonight," Daoin said. "I think I'm tired now, though. Is it all right if I sleep for a while? I don't want to miss the movie."

"Of course, Father. I'll make sure you do not miss it."

"Thank you. You're a good son." He smiled again. "I remember where my room is."

"Very good. I'm glad you remember."

"Goodnight...Taeral. And Gideon, and Sadie."

When he wandered out of the room, Taeral sagged in place. "He is getting worse," he murmured. "I must bring him across the Veil soon, or even Arcadia's magic will not be able to restore him."

"Then let's do it," I said. "We'll go now. Tonight, if you want to."

He huffed a breath. "I appreciate your enthusiasm, brother," he said. "But I cannot overstate the dangers we face. At the least, we should spend a few days to prepare so I can teach you to better wield your Fae magic. But even then the journey will pose a great risk to all of us."

"Yeah, you keep saying that. A lot," Sadie said. "That's why I'm going with you."

"Absolutely not."

"Yes, I am."

"No, you are not! I'll have enough trouble preventing them from detecting Daoin," he said. "I cannot protect you as well."

"Then you're missing the point," Sadie practically growled. "I'm not asking for your protection. I'm going to help protect *you*, and Gideon, and your father."

Taeral shook his head. "*A'ghreal*, please. Arcadia is no place for..."

"For what?" She was on her feet now, her eyes glittering. "A werewolf, or a woman?"

He lifted a hand toward her, then changed his mind and lowered it. "For the woman I cannot lose," he said.

"Taeral...do you really think I could stand to lose you? Either of you," she said, looking hard at me. "You guys just risked your lives to save my pack, and you didn't even know them. I *do* know you, and I'm *not* going to sit back while you rush off, and maybe die, when I could've done something to help. You got that?"

He looked away. "I'll consider it," he said. "That is the best I can offer."

"Well, you can damn well consider a better offer than no, because I'm not taking that one. I mean it." She glared at him for another moment, and then spun and left the room.

Taeral didn't move. Or speak. Eventually I said, "Maybe we should bring her. I mean, she's probably not going to let you leave her here."

"That is not her decision to make," he said through clenched teeth. "Nor is it yours."

"Fine. Maybe we shouldn't go at all, then," I said. "Because every time you bring it up, it sounds like an even worse idea than the last time."

"We have no choice."

"Hey, I can live without being a better DeathSpeaker. I don't even want this gig."

"And yet you have it," Taeral said flatly. "You can survive without the knowledge, yes. For a time. But what happens when a new branch of that blasted cult finds you, one with greater numbers or improved weapons? If you've no control over your abilities, Milus Dei will capture you. They will use you, break you down. And destroy all of us."

I shivered involuntarily. "There has to be another way."

"There is *no* other way! Not for you...and not for Daoin."

Suddenly I thought of what he'd said to Cobalt just before we left The Grotto. He'd thanked him for protecting me when he couldn't. And I remembered the damned promise, the one that condemned him to death if he failed to keep me safe to the best of his abilities. Under the current circumstances, helping me understand all this DeathSpeaker crap *was* keeping me safe.

So Arcadia was Taeral's only chance, too.

"Okay, look," I said. "If we have to, we have to. But I want to know something."

"What?" he said wearily.

"That promise you made. Is there any way to cancel it?" I said. "I mean, you said there's more magic in Arcadia. So is there a spell, or a magic potion or something, *anything* that keeps you from dying because of me?"

Taeral laughed without amusement. "Aye, there's a way. But it involves no magic—and it will never happen."

"What is it?"

"A promise can be pardoned, which negates the consequences of failure to keep it. But the pardon must be granted by a ruling King or Queen," he said. "I am Unseelie, so that leaves out the Seelie King. And the Unseelie Queen banished my father...so you can guess my chances of receiving a pardon from her."

Great. No matter what we did, we were screwed on that front.

And probably the rest of them, too.

CHAPTER 7

Movie night wasn't very well attended. None of the Duchenes had come down, and the other residents who occasionally came in for the show hadn't stirred from their rooms. Grygg, the massive golem who'd appointed himself guardian of the door, never joined us. The movie probably would've been over by the time he walked from the front desk to the parlor anyway.

I suspected everyone could feel the chill between Sadie and Taeral, and wanted nothing to do with the impending explosion.

Reun, Daoin, and Taeral occupied the front-and-center big couch. I sat on the loveseat next to it, and Sadie took the furthest possible chair back. Apparently, I'd been placed on the list of overprotective idiots by association. A few times I considered slipping back there to try talking to her, but the go-to-hell look on her face stopped me.

On the screen, Michael Corleone was in the bathroom at Louis, looking for the gun to carry out his first mission. But I wasn't paying much attention to the Godfather-in-training.

I was thinking about Arcadia.

From the first time I heard the word, I'd been drawn to it—even without knowing anything about the place. Taeral had only talked to me about it once. He hadn't said much. Just that the moon was eternal, brighter than it was here. That in the Fae realm, it was always night.

All my life, nights had been the best time for me. I felt safer under the moon. And there hadn't been much in the way of safety while I was growing up.

I didn't even need Taeral's constant reminders to know that Arcadia was a dangerous place. I could sense that myself, somehow. But part of me looked forward to going there, longed for it. And I had no idea why.

If Taeral really was going to help me figure out Fae magic, maybe I could get him to tell me a little more about the place. Like how to get there. I knew what crossing the Veil looked like, but only because of the Redcap who attacked me and Sadie in Central Park when we were looking for my mother's body. The thing that looked like a cross between a leprechaun and a vampire wanted to take me to the Unseelie Queen, for some reason. He'd opened a shimmering hole in reality and tried to drag me through.

I'd managed to bash him through it with a shovel like an angry, oversized softball instead, but I'd just about dislocated my arms doing it. The little biting bastard was heavier than he looked.

I dragged my attention back to the present. Daoin was completely absorbed in the movie, and Taeral was half-asleep. Reun watched the screen and Daoin at the same time. I glanced back and caught Sadie glaring at the back of Taeral's head.

We sure knew how to have fun around here.

Just as I was settling back, Daoin sat forward abruptly, startling Taeral into alertness. "Someone is coming," he said.

My breath caught. The last time he'd said that was a few seconds before Reun busted through the front door in a rage, demanding an audience with Daoin—back when we still thought the Seelie noble wanted to kill us.

And I wasn't the only one worried by the cryptic statement.

"Who?" Taeral said, looking wildly around the room. "Father, who is coming?"

Reun was already on his feet, moving toward the entrance to the parlor. "I will not allow them inside, whoever they are," he said.

"They've found me." Daoin stood, his gaze fastened on the television. "Taeral...run. Keep her safe."

Suddenly a jagged crack of light appeared on the screen, splitting Marlon Brando's jowled face in half. And a voice that definitely didn't belong to the Godfather boomed a single word.

"*Cíunaas.*"

My throat closed up tight. I tried to shout for Reun, to tell him I didn't think anyone was coming through the front door.

But I couldn't say a word. Sound refused to emerge from my mouth.

Just as I realized everyone else was suffering from the same problem, and the word had to be a spell, a figure emerged from the TV—heading straight for Daoin.

For one crazy second, I thought the Godfather had somehow stepped into the parlor.

But the figure was nothing like Brando. He was tall, slender, and definitely Fae, wearing something that looked like armor made of blue light. A pointed metal headband with a blue gemstone in the center rested on his high forehead, and Celtic-style tattoos decorated his face and neck.

The curved, serrated dagger carved with runes that he clutched in his hand looked sickeningly familiar. It was exactly the same as the one Taeral had given me—the one Daoin had made copies of when he was Captain of the Unseelie Guard.

It wasn't hard to deduce who this guy was.

Taeral lunged for Daoin, knocking him aside as the Fae from the portal dove at him. At the same time, another figure emerged...and another, and another, all of them identically dressed and similarly armed. Two of them grabbed Taeral. Just as he liberated a weapon from one of them and stabbed it through his assailant's arm, the other sank an identical dagger deep into his side.

His mouth opened in a silent scream as a third Fae soldier helped restrain him, and two more came through the shimmering rip. Then another. A pair of them had almost reached Daoin.

I lunged at the newest invader and managed to knock him down. He swiped his blade at me, but I grabbed his wrist, twisted and slammed. A snarl lifted his lip, showing pointed teeth as the knife clattered to the floor.

There was a flash of motion to my left—Sadie, charging into the fray around Taeral. Somewhere in the room, I heard a shouted spell that might have been Reun, and a powerful blast of air washed over me. The television smashed into the wall behind it in a shower of sparks.

But the soldiers were unaffected, and the rip remained.

And Taeral was being dragged through it.

No! I still couldn't speak. As I struggled with the Fae I'd pinned, two more rushed past us—then seconds later, I heard Reun scream. Sadie was on the floor, apparently unconscious. I refused to believe she was dead. And the soldier beneath me was almost free.

I drew an arm back and rammed a fist into his jaw.

He barely flinched. And then, he grinned. *"Tuariis'caen,"* he said.

The dagger I'd twisted away from him flew back into his hand, and in a single smooth motion, he plunged it through my shoulder.

Not being able to scream almost hurt more than the knife.

He pulled the blade free, flipped me off and scrambled upright. For an instant I got a good look at him—dark brown braided hair, gleaming amber-gold eyes, thorny vines tattooed across the bridge of his nose and around his throat like a collar. His grin chilled me to the core.

"Crohgaa," he said. *"Amaedahn...naech crohgaa."*

Whatever that meant, it wasn't a spell. I tried to stand, to go for him again, but only got halfway up before pain twisted through me and drove me to my knees. He grinned again, and dove through the portal.

I could only watch as the rest of them hauled an unresisting Daoin through the same way as Taeral—and the shimmering crack vanished.

CHAPTER 8

As soon as the portal closed, the invisible stranglehold on my throat released. "Sadie!" I gasped, dragging myself toward her motionless form. At least I could see her, and I could get to her.

I couldn't think about Taeral and Daoin yet. If I did, I'd lose it.

She was facedown with one arm flung over her head, and the other bent loosely behind her back. I moved to turn her over, momentarily forgetting about my shoulder until incredible pain surged through me and left my mouth in a hoarse scream.

Then I remembered the runes on those daggers were enchantments, designed to enhance the damage the weapons dealt.

My damage was definitely enhanced.

"Sadie..." I worked to flip her single-handed, dimly aware of the increased activity in the background that seem to come from another life. Motion and voices. I blocked them out and focused on Sadie.

She was breathing, at least. Her eyes were closed, and there was a small smear of blood at her right temple. I searched gently with my fingers, lifting her hair and feeling for injuries, before I realized that the blood was probably mine. My entire arm was soaked in blood that dripped from my fingertips.

But Sadie seemed untouched. They could've used the sleep spell on her—one of the few I actually knew. So maybe I could reverse it. Sometimes I could come up with Fae words I didn't know if I relaxed my focus, so I closed my eyes and tried not to think about how to say 'wake up.'

"*Diúsaegh.*"

I spoke the word almost before I thought it. Sadie's body stiffened, and her eyes flew open. "Taeral!" she called harshly, struggling to sit up. Her distant gaze barely registered me, even though I was right in front of her. "We have to stop them—"

"Sadie, wait." I grabbed her arm firmly, before she could bolt. "We can't."

Her lip curled as she wrenched away. "The hell we can't! Turn your pendant on," she said. "I'll go wolf and...kill every one of those..." Her voice faded as she finally looked around and realized how quiet it was. How the parlor wasn't full of Unseelie soldiers any more. How it was distinctly lacking Taeral. And Daoin—but she wasn't looking for him yet. "No," she said in a cracked whisper.

I shuddered and glanced over the rest of the room. Denei and Zoba, the two oldest Duchenes, were rushing toward Reun's sprawled and groaning form, half-propped against an overturned table. Two of their younger siblings stood near the parlor entrance, and Grygg was just outside it, glaring through angrily as one of the Duchenes spoke to him with rapid, emphatic gestures. None of them had seen what happened—it was over too fast.

"Gideon." Sadie's voice trembled. "Where is he? Where's Taeral?"

I wasn't sure I could speak. The weight of it threatened to crush me, the sick certainty that we'd never get them back. Those Fae had swatted every one of us down like insects in the space of two minutes, and there had to be a lot more where that batch came from. But she had to know. "I'm not sure," I managed. "But if I had to guess...I'd say Arcadia. Specifically, the Unseelie Court."

"You'd be right."

I barely recognized the splintered voice from across the room as Reun. He'd managed to stand with Denei supporting him, and now he limped toward us with an anguished expression. "They took both of them, didn't they? Daoin and Taeral."

I nodded, wincing at the fresh pain moving my neck caused.

"Oh, God," Sadie said. "We have to go after them."

"Who's them?" Denei demanded. "Reun, what the hell happened? Why didn't you call me down here?"

He eased himself straighter. "*They* are the Unseelie Guard. And you'd not have made it in time," he said. "This was carefully planned. The new moon, the precise location. They intended to neutralize, grab and leave."

"Well, when they come back, I'm damn sure gonna lay a hurt on 'em," she said.

Just behind her, Zoba made a very unpleasant sound. I could only assume he agreed.

"They'll not return. They have what they came for." Reun stepped away from her, his hand lingering on her arm for a moment. Apparently the two of them still had a thing together, though I couldn't imagine the attraction. "Gideon, your shoulder," he said. "A *drais-ghan*?"

It took me a few seconds to puzzle that one out. Spelled dagger. "Yeah, that," I said. I decided not to mention it was a copy of the one Reun's wife had given to Daoin while they were having an affair. No need to rub that in at the moment.

"Jesus!" Sadie scrambled to her feet. "You're bleeding all over the place. Why didn't you say something?"

"Thought it was kind of obvious." I was still on my knees, and I wasn't sure I could get up. The slightest movement made my whole arm feel like it was going to explode.

She bent closer to look at the wound. "How bad is it?" she said, reaching for my shoulder.

"Don't—"

She touched it. And I screamed.

Sadie snatched her hand back fast. "Sorry. I guess that means pretty bad, right?"

"Good guess," I ground out.

Reun stepped up beside me and knelt. "I can remove the enchantment," he said. "But I'll not be able to heal it completely. And it will hurt."

I managed a weak laugh. "Can't hurt more than it already does."

"Actually, it can."

"Great," I sighed. "Well, go for it anyway."

"Hold on." Denei made her way over, working something free from the pocket of her tight leather pants. I half expected one of her voodoo pouches. But what she produced was a block of wood about the size of a small candy bar, wrapped with flat strips of leather. "Bite down on this, handsome," she said. "It'll help."

I wasn't even going to ask why she carried something like that around with her. Or why it already had teeth marks in it.

Without asking whether I agreed, she shoved it in my mouth. So I bit down, closed my eyes, and waited.

It did hurt more. A lot more.

Just as I was sure I'd bite the damned wood block in half and pass out choking on the splinters, the blinding pain eased to a sharp ache. I opened my eyes in time to see Reun sag back, panting. "I've done all I can," he said. "But now the rest will heal on its own."

I used my non-stabbed arm to take the block out of my mouth and wiped it awkwardly on my shirt. "Uh, thanks," I said, handing it back to Denei. "Both of you, I mean."

Reun nodded and stood slowly. "I've failed to protect Lord Daoin," he said, his voice still hoarse with pain. "I must redeem myself. The Unseelie Court may be willing to exchange his life for mine."

"Whoa. Hold on," I said, finally managing to stand. "No one's exchanging anyone's life. We'll find another way, and we will get them back." My gut twisted as the words left my mouth. I had no idea how to do that, and I didn't actually think we had a chance in hell of succeeding.

But if I had to, I'd die trying.

"We cannot defeat the Unseelie Guard." Reun broke away and moved toward the busted television, staring at the still-smoldering heap of plastic and metal. "Negotiation is the only way."

Denei bared her teeth at him. "Don't you even think like that," she said. "You ain't dying for him. All of us together, we can take on a bunch of Fae *cochon*."

"No. We can't." He gave her a sad smile. "It was an honor to know you, *a'stohr*. And…I am sorry I could not protect you all."

"Reun!"

In the space it took Denei to call his name, he gestured a gleaming rip into existence and stepped through.

It vanished along with him.

CHAPTER 9

"Goddamn it!" Denei glared at the space where Reun was, her amber eyes burning. After a few seconds, she shook herself and spun on a heel. "We gon' find a way to follow that stubborn son of a whore, like it or not. Come, Zoba," she spat as she marched across the room.

For once, Zoba didn't make a sound. He just shook his head and followed his sister.

Sadie clapped a hand to her mouth, staggered to the nearest couch and sat down hard. "We can't save them," she whispered through her fingers. "Can we? They're really...gone."

"No, they're not." I settled beside her carefully, mindful of my still-throbbing shoulder. "I wasn't kidding. We'll get them back." *Somehow.*

She lowered her hand and stared at me with glittering eyes. "How?" There was a shrill edge to her voice that was very close to panic. "They're in *Arcadia*. We can't exactly take the goddamned train there! And the only person who could've brought us across the Veil just basically committed suicide." Her chest heaved once. "Even if we could get there, how the hell are we going to find them, let alone fight a bunch of Fae warriors? I mean, I don't know about you, but I have no idea where the Unseelie Court is."

"I don't either," I admitted. "But I know how we can get to Arcadia."

She shuddered. "You can't guess at this one, Gideon," she said. "Who knows what'll happen if you get it wrong? You could end up transporting us to Mars or something. Or just flat-out kill us both."

SONYA BATEMAN

"Then it's a good thing I'm not guessing." This morning already seemed so long ago, but I remembered thinking I'd never take the offer because Taeral would kill me for it. Now it might be the only way to save him—though I doubted he'd find the irony amusing. "We're going to ask Cobalt for help."

Sadie caught a breath. "Do you really think he will?"

"He said if we needed a resource, he'd do what he could. I think this qualifies," I said.

"Let's go, then." She took my hand, and I could feel her trembling. "Right now. Will said they're night people, didn't he? So maybe they're still awake."

The hope in her eyes nearly killed me. Even if we did make it to Arcadia, she was right about the rest of it. We'd never find the Unseelie Court—I didn't even know what it was, let alone where to start looking for it. And what chance did one lone werewolf and one halfling Fae, who barely knew how to cast a sleep spell, have against a bunch of full-powered, trained Unseelie fighters?

I almost wished we'd saved some of that bio-drug Milus Dei created to use against us. The one that suppressed the human part and left only the Other. I'd hated what I became when I used it—a cold, calculating killer with no regard, no hesitation, and no remorse.

But I had to admit, a bloodthirsty Fae would've been a lot more helpful than me in this particular case.

"All right," I finally said. "Let's go."

———————◆———————

This time I knew where the place was, so I drove my van.

I'd taken care of a few things before we left the Castle. Not that I wanted to think this way, but I had to act like I was never coming back. So I'd half-ass bandaged my arm, swapped my bloody shirt for a fresh one, and rearranged a few things in my room. And while Sadie packed a bag, I'd had a talk with Grygg—assuring him that it wasn't his fault, and asking him to keep protecting the place. I didn't tell him exactly where we were going, in case Denei tried to follow.

But I did tell him that if a certain police captain showed up at the hotel, he should let him in and show him to my room. Because there was an uncomfortable conversation I needed to have with Abe before we left.

I parked in a garage about a block away from The Grotto and paid for a full week in advance. Figured if we weren't back by then, I'd probably be dead and I wouldn't care what happened to my van. It wasn't exactly a comforting thought, but I seemed to be fresh out of optimism.

Hell, maybe Abe could use the van. After the modifications Chester Rigby made while we were in the mountains, it'd make a great SWAT vehicle.

He wasn't going to like that suggestion, either.

It was going on midnight when Sadie and I walked up to the plain metal door in the plain brick wall. At least the building hadn't disappeared again since this morning. I kind of felt bad coming here so late, even if they were still awake. But I figured this qualified as an emergency. Hopefully, Cobalt would understand.

"Well," I said, resting a hand on the push bar. "Guess I'll knock?" Almost absently, I leaned on the bar and pushed the door a little.

And just about fell through it when it opened.

"What the…" Frowning, I glanced at Sadie. "He can't still be open for business. Who gets tattoos at midnight?"

"Who cares," she said. "It's not locked. Let's just go in."

"Right." I opened the door the rest of the way and stepped into the entry room, with Sadie right behind me.

This time, there was someone sitting at the wooden table.

I didn't recognize the guy. East Indian, maybe twenty years old, and watching us with veiled caution. His gaze kept flicking to the wall—and I realized I'd set the alarm system glowing again.

"Um. Hi," I said. The kid seemed human, but I couldn't make assumptions one way or the other. "Didn't know you were still open…are you?"

"Yes. But we don't have any more appointments scheduled tonight," he said with another glance at the glowing runes. "Are you expected?"

"Not exactly. But I really need to see Cobalt."

"I don't think—"

Just then, the right-hand door across the small room opened. The man who stepped out was blond-haired, green-eyed, and wore a sweater and pressed slacks. He grinned at me like a long-lost friend. "Hey there," he said in a rich brogue. "Just the two of you, then?"

"Uh…"

The kid glanced at the blond. "Were you expecting them?"

"Not so much, but they're a welcome surprise," the man said. "They're all right, Malik. Cobalt knows them."

"Okay, I guess. But we're not going to have any…er, fun like last time, are we?"

"Nah. I think we're good." The blond walked toward me, extending a hand. "I'm Nix," he said. "Pleasure to meet you, mate."

Despite my extreme confusion, I shook automatically. "Do I know you?" I blurted.

"Not yet." He turned the grin on Sadie. "Welcome," he said. "I can see you've something important on your mind. Come in, please. We'll make sure you get sorted."

Sadie blinked a few times. "Who's we?" she said. "Are you—"

"Ah, best come inside first. Then we'll chat," Nix said, raising a hand to Malik as he opened the door he'd come through. "No worries, mate," he said. "Job well done. I'll take full responsibility for them."

Malik frowned. "If you say so."

"You know I'm good for it," he said, and then smiled at me. "Coming?"

Sadie and I exchanged a look, and followed him through the door—into something that had about as much in common with a tattoo studio as my van did with a Lamborghini.

The place looked like a nightclub. Round tables with three or four chairs apiece filled most of the floor space in the vast, low-lit room, and about half of them were occupied by people. Each table had a velvet-bound book fastened to the center with a slender chain. One lay open on a nearby table, revealing pages of photographed body art. Music played from somewhere overhead and mingled with the hum of conversation. Instead of a bar, there was a row of high-end vending machines to the left, offering coffee and cappuchino, water and health drinks, cold and hot food, and restaurant-style desserts.

Three lit glass booths stood at the far end of the room. Inside them were tattoo benches, tattoo equipment—and people currently getting tattoos, while everyone else in the room watched.

I found myself glad Cobalt didn't have this place when I went to him the first time. I never would've been able to do that in front of an audience.

Nix led us to a table ahead and off to the right, in a kind of nook that was more or less separate from the rest of the place. Someone was already seated there—not Cobalt, since I was pretty sure he was in the center booth. When we got close enough, I made out an incredibly striking woman with pale skin, dark eyes, jet-black hair and delicate features.

And whoever she was, she didn't look happy to see us.

"You were right, love. As usual." Nix stopped and gestured at the woman. "My wife, Shade," he said.

Wife? I managed to stop myself from blurting aloud. They seemed a little mismatched.

The woman looked hard at me. "Appearances can be deceiving."

I actually felt my jaw drop.

Nix burst out laughing. "I do love watching you work, my heart," he said. "It's just priceless, every time. Shall we see it again?"

Sadie elbowed me. "What's going on?" she hissed.

"Um." I had to make a conscious effort not to step back. "I think...Shade...is psychic."

"Aye, she is," Nix said.

Sadie's eyes narrowed. "Hey. I don't want anyone poking around in my head," she said, that shrill, almost-panic edge back in her tone. "Don't even think about...thinking at me, or whatever you do."

"You've nothing to worry about. I can only hear what wants to be heard." Shade stared calmly at her for a moment, and then turned to Nix. "Are you going to introduce them?"

"Well. Haven't exactly caught their names yet, myself."

Shade rolled her eyes. "You are a hopeless knob."

"Aye, but I'm *your* knob," he said with a grin. "Besides, I can guess. You'd be Sadie. And since you're not attempting to kill me, you must be Gideon."

"Yeah, that's us," I said weakly. Jesus Christ. How many Fae hung around this place anyway? Cobalt, his terrifying brother, and now these two. "Are you psychic too?"

"Not a bit. Cobalt mentioned the visit this morning," Nix said. "He thought you might be back sometime, so he asked that we keep an eye out for you. Then Shade sensed your presence, and here we all are. Cozy as peas."

Sadie blew out a breath. "That's great. But we need to talk to Cobalt," she said. "It's important."

"Yes, he's noticed." Shade cast a glance toward the glass booths. "And he'll join us directly."

"But—"

"Sadie." I took her hand gently, and a lump formed in my throat. She was still shaking. "Please, try to relax. A little," I said. "We'll get through this. But we can't do anything....crazy right now. Understand?"

For a minute I thought she would anyway. Like start screaming, or punch me and then start screaming. But she closed her eyes and swallowed once, and her spine stiffened. "You're right," she said. "I just…"

I squeezed her hand. "I know."

With a sobered expression, Nix pulled the chair closest to Sadie away from the table. "All right. Sit down," he said. "Please. Before you fall."

She looked at him blankly, then shivered and lowered herself into the seat.

Shade watched me as I sat in the chair between her and Sadie. Her eyes widened a touch. "You're bleeding," she said in a surprisingly soft tone.

"Huh?" At first I thought she was doing the psychic thing again, until I glanced down and saw the dark, wet spot seeping into my shirt. Probably should've taken a bit more time with the bandage. "Er, yeah," I said. "A little."

"That's not a little."

Nix made a low, distressed sound. "I'm sorry, mate," he said. "Hadn't realized you were that bad off. I can go fetch Cobalt—"

"No need," a new voice said.

I breathed an inward sigh of relief. Finally, someone I knew. Sort of.

Cobalt came up beside Nix, looking from Sadie to me with concern. "I'd ask if everything was all right, but I can see it's not," he said. "Your brother hasn't joined you tonight?"

A wrenching sob escaped Sadie before she could cover her mouth.

"Ah, so that's it." Cobalt turned a calm expression to Nix. "Tell Malik we're closing early," he said. "Can you help him clear the place and lock up, and then meet us upstairs?"

"On it, mate." Nix immediately headed back the way we'd come in.

"Don't worry," Cobalt said to me. "We can talk in private. And I'll heal that arm of yours, too—it looks bad."

I frowned. "We weren't trying to mess up your business," I said. "I mean, you don't have to do all this."

"Of course I do. You need help." He gave an encouraging smile. "It's no trouble," he said. "I meant what I said earlier. If I can help you, I will."

I almost started crying myself. "Thank you," I managed.

One step down. And countless, impossible steps to go.

CHAPTER 10

The reactions I got after I explained what happened didn't exactly inspire me with hope.

We were in Cobalt's apartment. Sadie and I on one couch; Cobalt, Nix and Shade on the other. Will was at work. Cobalt had mentioned he usually didn't get home until one or two, depending on how much post-show stuff he had. I'd just given them the short version—basically, the Unseelie Guard teleporting through The Godfather and dragging Taeral and Daoin back to Arcadia with them.

All three of them looked horrified.

Cobalt was the first to speak. "I must call Uriskel," he said, dragging a hand down his face as he stood.

"Er. Must you?"

His disappointed look made me regret the words. But I couldn't help it—his brother scared the shit out of me. "Yes, I must," he said. "Uriskel knows more of the Unseelie Court than all of us together. "Believe me when I say that you'll need his counsel, at the least. If he'll consent to offer it."

I let out a sigh. "I believe you. And I'm sorry," I said. "Look, I've only known about all this Other stuff for a couple of months, including that I'm Fae. I mean, half Fae. And your brother is...really badass. That's all."

"Months?" Cobalt's expression softened. "I assumed you'd known for years," he said. "*I'm* sorry for that. And I'll only ask that you be patient with Uriskel." He closed his eyes briefly. "He's a good heart, but my brother has been through...difficulties, which are not my place to discuss."

Without knowing it, he'd just told me a whole lot about his brother. I recognized abuse when people were trying to hide it. So maybe I could give him the benefit of the doubt—for now, at least. "I can do that," I said.

"Thank you. Please, excuse me for a moment."

Cobalt walked away, and I glanced at Sadie with concern. She hadn't said a word since we came up here. At the moment, she was staring toward the big window and the glittering sprawl of Manhattan beyond—but I doubted she was seeing any of it.

I patted her leg, and she stirred and gave me a slight smile. At least she was still in there somewhere.

"So," I said to the odd couple. "You guys are Fae, right?"

Nix smiled crookedly. "Nah, we're bloody unicorns," he said. "Course we are."

"Oh." I wondered if there was a tactful way to ask if they were Seelie or Unseelie. Taeral always seemed to know, but I was still having trouble figuring out whether someone was human or not.

Then I remembered Shade could hear thoughts that wanted to be heard. Maybe if I thought hard enough, I wouldn't have to ask what was probably a stupid question out loud.

Just as the idea crossed my mind, she raised an elegant eyebrow. "It's not a stupid question," she said. "But it is something of a complicated answer."

"Holy shit. You heard me?"

"Aye. You wanted me to, didn't you?" She actually smiled a little, and even Sadie took notice. "We're not high Fae, Nix and I," she said. "At least, that is the term, though I've never agreed with it. High Fae, pure Seelie and Unseelie, control the Summer and Winter Courts. But there are many other...variations, all of us labeled low Fae."

"You mean like Redcaps," I said. That's what Sadie had called the pointy-toothed leprechaun—a low Fae.

Nix stared at me. "You've seen a Redcap?" he said. "Here?"

61

"Er, yeah. Once," I said. "Long story."

"Don't interrupt, you daft bit," Shade said, not unkindly. "They should know this."

He grinned. "Sorry, love. I'm an insensitive tool, a bloody flake, and so forth."

"That you are." She shook her head. "As I was saying, there are many types of low Fae. Dryads, nymphs, Redcaps, gnomes, brownies. My thick-headed mate here is a Pooka, and I am Sluagh. And we, the low Fae, are Seelie or Unseelie depending on where in Arcadia our kind dwells, and which Court's rule we're subjected to." Her lingering smile slipped away. "Meaning he's Seelie, and I'm Unseelie."

"Aye. Arcadia forbids the union of Seelie and Unseelie—it's the one thing both Courts agree on." Nix took his wife's hand gently. "That's why we're here, instead of there."

Damn. I knew they didn't get along, but this seemed somehow worse than killing each other. It sounded like the high Fae had basically forced a bunch of other Fae who didn't have anything to do with them to take sides, and then made loyalty a requirement. "So you couldn't be together at all over there?" I said.

"We couldn't *survive* there," Shade said. "The penalty for such a union is death."

I decided not to ask what the Courts' policies were on human-Fae unions. Figured I could probably guess.

Before I could horrify myself further, Cobalt returned from wherever he'd gone, tucking a phone in his pocket. "Coincidentally, Uriskel is aware that you're here," he said. "And despite swearing he'd no longer protect me when I don't need it, he's already on the way. He'll be here momentarily."

"Fantastic," Nix said. "Your brother's presence always livens the place up. I'll nip down and let him in, shall I?"

"Please do. I'd rather he didn't break my door down. Again."

Nix stood and headed for the stairs. And I tried to stay calm, reminding myself that at least I had a vague idea why Uriskel acted the way he did.

Unfortunately, it didn't make him any less terrifying.

When Uriskel joined us, I had to repeat my little story. But he wasn't satisfied with 'a bunch of angry fairies came through the TV and stole my father and brother.'

"You must know *something*." Once again, the red-haired Unseelie had refused to sit down. He stood at the end of the longer couch, staring at me in disgust—like he'd just decided he owned underwear that was smarter than me. "Why would the Unseelie Guard want your brother?"

"Look, I have no idea," I said. "I'm pretty sure they were after Daoin, and they only took Taeral because he was there."

"Daoin?" Uriskel said hoarsely.

"Yeah, Taeral's—well, our father. He's supposed to be banished, so I don't know why they'd take him back."

"Lord Daoin Ciar' Ansghar, Captain of the Unseelie Guard." Uriskel took a menacing step forward. "*That* is your father?"

I tried to shrink into the couch. "Look, I don't know anything about him," I said. "I just met the guy a few months ago, and he was already..."

"Already what?" he demanded.

"Gone, okay?" I nearly shouted. This was starting to piss me off. I lunged to my feet and paced toward the window, my hands clenched tight. "Whoever Daoin was before, he's not anymore. He hasn't been for a long time," I said without turning. "He doesn't remember anything about his life, and he barely remembers Taeral is his son. Hell, he doesn't know who *he* is half the time. So I don't fucking understand why the Unseelie Court came for him, but I'm getting both of them back, damn it!"

A resounding silence answered my rant, and I looked back to find everyone gaping at me. Including Uriskel.

"What's happened to him?" Uriskel said in an almost normal tone.

I released a pent breath. "You guys ever hear of Milus Dei?"

"Gideon, don't." Sadie sat forward with an alarmed expression. "We shouldn't talk about that."

"Yeah, we should." I knew what had her worried. If they found out what I was, besides half Unseelie, they might not help us—because there was a distinct possibility Milus Dei would target them, too. But I wasn't going to let anyone risk their lives without knowing what they were getting into. "Have you heard of it?" I repeated.

Cobalt frowned. "Aye, but only rumors," he said. "They're supposed to be some kind of cult looking to destroy all non-humans. The men of legend—and I'd assumed that's what they were. Legends, stories to frighten children."

"Well, they're real." I crossed my arms and focused on nothing in particular. "Milus Dei is what happened to Daoin," I said. "They held him captive for twenty-six years. Kept him in a room with cold iron walls, experimented on him, tortured him. When we got him out of there, they'd left him to bleed to death—he had no magic left, so he couldn't heal himself."

I could barely look at their stricken expressions. At least they believed me.

Sadie got up and walked over to me. "They had Taeral too, for almost a year," she said. "That's how he lost his arm. And they caught me twice."

"Where is this Milus Dei?" Uriskel said.

I frowned. "Good question. We fought them, thought we'd stopped them—but then we found out the group in New York was only a branch," I said. "Apparently they're all over the world. We just got back from fighting another bunch of those bastards in Pennsylvania. They'd taken Sadie's pack."

"My God, I'm so sorry," Cobalt rasped. "Gideon, you said you'd only known about the Others, and your own heritage, for a few months. Is *this* how you found out?"

"Yeah. They came after me pretty hard, so I had to figure everything out fast—and not die while I was doing it."

Uriskel raised an eyebrow. "If you'd not known what you are, why did they come after you?" he said.

Of course he'd ask that.

Sadie mouthed *no*, but I had to tell them. And if they weren't willing to help, we'd find another way. I drew a steadying breath and looked directly at the Unseelie.

"Because I'm the DeathSpeaker."

CHAPTER 11

Uriskel stared at me so intensely, I started to think I'd burst into flames any second. Finally, he said. "I will accompany you to Arcadia, to save your family."

Okay. That was definitely not what I expected to hear.

Before I could react, Cobalt blurted, "No. You can't go back there, Uri."

"Why not? Because they'll kill me?"

"Yes!"

"Well, they've not managed it yet."

"Uh, guys?" I was still trying to process the idea that Uriskel had offered to help save Taeral, and so far I'd only come to one conclusion—having him on my side was even scarier. "No one has to go with us," I said. "We just need help getting there."

"Really," Uriskel said. "You'll go to Arcadia, with no knowledge of the place or its people, and challenge the Unseelie Court for their prisoners. Even though neither of you will be welcomed there, and you'll both be hunted down and likely killed."

"Yeah, I will."

He made a gesture at me. "You see?" he said to Cobalt. "*That* is why I must go."

Cobalt drew himself straight and glared at his brother. "Let me go, then," he said. "I agree they must have a guide, if he's truly the DeathSpeaker. But not you."

"And what do you know of the Unseelie Court, *brother?*"

"Enough to know they'll destroy you, or worse!"

Uriskel responded with a sharp, rapid string of Fae that I couldn't follow at all. I really wished I knew the language. Whatever he said, it turned Cobalt white as a sheet.

"Very well," Cobalt said in rough tones. "But what am I supposed to tell Trystan?"

"I'll tell him myself." There was a slight catch in Uriskel's voice, but he recovered quickly and looked at me. "Did you have any particular strategy for how to rescue them, DeathSpeaker?" he said.

"Not really. We...Taeral was planning on having us go to Arcadia soon. He wanted to try healing Daoin there, and we were supposed to talk to someone who knew the previous DeathSpeaker," I said. "Because honestly, I have no idea what I'm doing. I don't even know how to be Fae, much less the DeathSpeaker."

"Fantastic," he muttered. "Who did he intend to speak with?"

I shrugged. "He didn't exactly say."

"Perhaps the Sluagh knows." Uriskel half-turned toward the couch with a raised brow. "Well? Any ideas, oh mistress of darkness?"

I finally realized that Nix had gone completely silent and unsmiling, and Shade looked extremely distressed. "The DeathSpeaker," she whispered. "You're certain of this?"

"Yeah. Unless there's some other way to make dead people talk," I said.

"Gideon...do you know what happened to the last DeathSpeaker?"

"Not a clue."

"He went insane and slaughtered hundreds in Arcadia," she said. "He created the Wasteland—left a scar on the realm, burned of all magic. And it took more than two dozen of the most powerful high Fae to bring him down. If you cross the Veil, and anyone realizes what you are..."

My stomach lurched at the idea that anyone could do that. "But I'm not him," I said.

"It doesn't matter. Simply being the DeathSpeaker is enough to condemn you." She turned a solemn gaze to Sadie. "There's danger for you, as well. Something happens to werefolk in Arcadia. They become…unstable."

"All right. Enough with the prattling, crystal-ball warnings," Uriskel said dryly. "Do you know who the Unseelie would have spoken to, or not?"

"Hey, what's your problem?" I said. "And how would she know what Taeral was thinking, anyway?"

He glowered at me. "Because her kind worships death. If there's anyone in Arcadia who might've had a favorable relationship with the lunatic who held your position before you, it's a Sluagh."

"We commune with spirits," Shade said, glaring right back at him. "And yes, I've an idea. You can be polite if you'd like to hear it, Uriskel, or you'll need to buy me more than a drink to keep me from spilling your little secrets."

"Fine," he groaned. "Shade, would you be so kind as to share with me who we might speak to about the DeathSpeaker?"

Sadie managed a smile at that. "Oh, I like you," she said to Shade.

"I've plenty of experience dealing with manly fools," Shade said. "I'm sure you've had your share, as well."

"Oh, yeah."

"Hey," I said. "Why do I get the feeling you're talking about me?"

Sadie shrugged. "You must be psychic, too."

"At any rate," Shade said with a crooked smile. "The one you'd be looking for is probably Nyantha. My grand-aunt, coincidentally. You'll find her in the marshlands, likely around the Trees of Ankou."

"Where we'll wander for days, no doubt," Uriskel grumbled.

"Really, must I explain everything to you?" Shade let out a nearly playful huff. "Nyantha is psychic. Just think of your need to speak with her, and she'll find you."

"Of course. Thank you," Uriskel said stiffly. "Now, the two of you rest tonight, and we'll depart in the morning."

"Uriskel," Cobalt said haltingly.

"What is it now?"

He opened his mouth, and closed it again. "Just...swear you'll come back," he said. "I can't lose you like this again."

Uriskel deflated a bit, then reached out and clasped his shoulder. "You know I can't promise that, brother. But I've no intention of dying—or letting these two noble imbeciles get themselves killed."

"I suppose if that's the best you've got..." With a sad smile, Cobalt took his other shoulder. "Well met, then."

"Well met." Uriskel nodded and lowered his hand. "All right, enough grousing. I've got to get home and..." He shivered slightly. "I'll return in the morning."

"Uriskel, wait," I said.

He stared at me. "*Now* what?"

"Why are you doing this?" I had no idea what happened before, but I felt awful watching him say goodbye to his brother. And apparently there was someone at home he was leaving behind, too. "You don't know me, or Sadie, and you hate Taeral. You know who Daoin is, but it doesn't seem like you think much of him, either," I said. "Look, I don't want to die— but I definitely don't want someone else doing it for me."

He actually smiled. A little. "You've just said why I'm doing it, right there. Besides the fact that you're the DeathSpeaker, and you must be protected...you would die for your brother. That alone earns my respect." He glanced at Cobalt, and added, "I've some experience in that regard."

"Aye, and he's a damned stubborn fool," Cobalt said.

"At least I'm not a great softhearted dolt." Uriskel smirked, lifted a hand in parting and headed for the stairs.

"Rise early," he called over his shoulder. "We've much ground to cover, before we attempt to face the Winter Court."

Great. Now I kind of liked Uriskel.

And that only made everything a hell of a lot worse.

CHAPTER 12

Cobalt invited us to stay in his guest room for the night. It was a better idea than sleeping in my van, or going back to the Castle—if I talked to Denei before we left, she'd insist on going with us. And I didn't want to risk any more lives than we already were.

I hadn't even told any of them about Reun yet. Probably should do that in the morning.

The emotional shock had driven Sadie to exhaustion. She was barely on her feet when Cobalt showed us to the room. I helped her into the queen bed over her half-mumbled protests that she wanted to leave now, and her eyes closed the instant her head hit the pillow. The room also had an overstuffed chair. I'd sleep in that, because I had to get up earlier than her. There was someone I needed to talk to before I went to a place I might never come back from.

And he was going to be pissed.

I fired off a text to Abe, figuring he'd definitely be asleep by now, and asked if we could meet up early for coffee. Then I tossed the phone on the chair and used the small bathroom attached to the guest room. When I came back out, I had a reply.

You never get up early. What's wrong? Call me.

Guess he wasn't asleep after all.

I had to close my eyes for a minute before I dialed him. Of all the "fathers" I had, Abraham Strauss was the closest one to a dad. He'd brought me to the fosters I stayed with after I escaped the Valentines, kept me in school and out of trouble, supported me while I went to community college. After graduation, when I failed at being a paramedic and decided body moving was the career for me, he'd helped me get gigs with the NYPD. He'd been there for everything that mattered in my life.

And I had no idea how to tell him that I wasn't entirely human, or that I was going to a magical realm he couldn't get to, where I might die.

Abe answered on the first ring. "Where are you?"

"Hey, Captain," I said, trying to keep my tone light. "I'm fine. How are you?"

"Gideon, it's one in the morning. You're not fine."

Damn. Always the detective, even though he'd been promoted. "I am fine, though," I said. At this very moment, I was not in any physical danger. But I wouldn't explain the technicalities that way. "I just...need to talk to you. In person."

"Are you going to fight another pack of werewolves?" he said. "Thanks for the heads-up on that, by the way. It was great finding out from the local sheriff of East Nowhere."

"Yeah, sorry about that. And no, not fighting werewolves." I sighed and rubbed the back of my neck. "I don't want to talk about this on the phone," I said. I owed him more than that. "So, how about we have coffee? Say six, at that diner by the precinct?"

"How about we talk now? I'm already awake. Where are you?"

Great. I really hadn't wanted to tell him this before I saw him. "You know that suspicious tattoo shop you said I should probably stay away from?"

He groaned. "Let me guess. You're there."

"Gold star, Detective. I mean Captain."

"Fine. I'll be there in fifteen."

"Abe—"

"Too late. I'm already worried." His smirk translated loud and clear through the phone. "See you soon. I'll even bring coffee, but it's gonna be that crappy gas station stuff."

"That works," I said. "Thanks, Abe."

I ended the call and hesitated before I left the room. Cobalt had probably gone to bed, and I didn't want to disturb him. But I also didn't want to screw with the entrance to the place and make him think there was a break-in or something.

Fortunately, it turned out I didn't have to worry. Cobalt and Will were sitting on the loveseat, talking in hushed tones when I came out.

"Er. Sorry," I said when they both looked up. "A friend of mine is on the way here. I needed to talk to him before...you know, and he insisted on doing it now. I was just going to wait outside for him."

Cobalt frowned. "It's freezing outside," he said. "You can talk in the studio, if you'd like some privacy. Is your friend Unseelie?"

"Nah, he's human."

"Then I'll not have to invite him inside. If you'll just lock up when you're through, I'd appreciate it."

"No problem. Uh, thanks," I said. "Hey, Will. Sorry about crashing the place."

"It's fine," Will said with a smile. "Cobalt did the same thing for me when I needed it."

I couldn't help a wry laugh. Somehow I doubted Will had needed to rescue his family from evil fairies—but I appreciated the sentiment. "Listen, about your brother..."

Cobalt waved me off. "Once Uriskel's decided on a course of action, there's no force in any realm to stop him," he said. "I don't like him risking his life, but I don't blame you at all. This was his decision." One corner of his mouth lifted slightly. "And he may actually have a way for all of you to come through this intact, though he'll have to be the one to tell you. If he so chooses."

"Great." He must've meant whatever Uriskel said in Fae that made him change his mind. Plans I didn't know anything about were my favorite—especially when they were made by a terrifying Unseelie. "Well, anyway...thank you," I said. "I'd better get down there. He'll freak out if I'm not where I said I'd be."

"Very well." Cobalt nodded. "Goodnight, Gideon."

"'Night."

I waved and rushed down the stairs, already fighting a swell of frustrated panic.

How could I tell Abe that I might never see him again?

———————◆●◆———————

"I knew it," Abe said.

We were sitting at one of the tables in the studio, drinking coffee that was as terrible as he'd threatened. With the lights on and the people gone, the place was kind of creepy.

I still hadn't gotten to any of the actual bad news, and Abe was already upset.

"Hey, I'm not fighting werewolves," I said. I'd only told him that I had to go away for a while. "It's not even Milus Dei this time."

"So what is it?"

Worse. I took a swallow of overcooked coffee and managed not to gag. "It's like this," I said. "You know Taeral?"

His brow furrowed. "Your friend with the metal arm. The, uh, Fae."

"Yeah, him. Thing is...he's not my friend." I stared at the table for a minute, and finally got enough nerve to look at Abe. "He's my brother."

I could see the moment it clicked into place for him. "Your actual brother?" he said.

"Well, half-brother." Abe knew the Others existed—he'd met most of them I knew, under seriously strained circumstances. But I had the feeling it was all kind of philosophical for him. Until now. "I didn't know anything about it until I met him, a few days before you did," I said. "That's when I found out we have the same birth father. His name is Daoin...and he's Fae."

Abe frowned slightly. "Was it an affair or something? I thought you lived with your parents."

"Yeah. So did I." This part got a little unbelievable, so I tried to explain it as simply as possible. "Apparently my real mother died when I was born, and I was switched at birth."

"Huh," he said. "Isn't that the damndest thing? I never thought that switched-at-birth stuff really happened."

It wasn't exactly a traditional switch, but I wouldn't get into that right now. "I gotta say, you're taking this really well."

"Taking what well?"

"Seriously, Abe?" I said. "I just told you I'm not human."

He looked surprised. And then, he smiled. "Werewolf, Fae, bogeyman, whatever—we're all basically people," he said. "Well, maybe not the bogeyman. Point is, I wouldn't care if you were part chupacabra, Gideon. I know you. You're a good kid...a good man. And you've saved a lot of lives. Including mine, in case you forgot." He reached across the table and patted my hand. "That makes you human in my book."

My throat spasmed shut. Right then, I almost decided not to go through with it.

But if I didn't, I wouldn't be the man he thought I was. The man I wanted to be.

"Thank you." I drew a deep breath, and it shuddered out of me in a rush. There was no easing into this. I'd just have to spit it out. "Taeral and Daoin were kidnapped by some very bad Fae who aren't going to let them go, and probably plan to kill them," I said. "So we have to go try to rescue them—me and Sadie, and another Fae. But these guys took them to Arcadia. The Fae realm. It's...not exactly on Earth, and we have to use magic to get there. And I might not make it back."

Abe didn't say anything for a long time. He stared at me, sipped his coffee, and stared some more. At last he pushed the cup away and said, "Yes, you will."

75

"Abe, don't—"

"You will." He shook his head, and a grim smile formed on his lips. "Even if you might not, just make an old man happy and lie to me. Say you will."

"All right," I said slowly, not sure I'd be able to keep talking like this. But I pressed on somehow. "I will, then. Be back in about a week, maybe less. But in case I'm...late..."

"We're lying here, remember?"

"In case I'm late," I said firmly. I couldn't leave without telling him this. "I told you about Chester Rigby, and how he's been digging into Milus Dei for years."

"The town nutcase out in Pennsylvania. Yeah, I remember," Abe said.

"Well, he's not completely crazy. He's right about everything but the aliens." I laughed in spite of myself. Chester had managed to convince himself that the cult was a carefully planned, long-term alien invasion, trying to create a race of genetic super-soldiers. But he did have a lot of information on their history, branches, and current locations—and he'd given me copies of everything. "Anyway, I have tons of stuff on these guys. It's in my room, at the place I told you I was staying," I said. "If I'm late, I'd like you to go there and get it. They know you might be coming. Who knows, maybe the NYPD can do something about those bastards. Now that one of them isn't running it."

Abe let out a heavy sigh. "Fine. But it's not going to be necessary," he said. "When you get back, we can both work on it."

"Yeah. We'll do that." I grimaced and reached into my pocket. "One more thing," I said, putting my van keys and the parking garage ticket on the table. "It's in the E-Z Park at Eighth and Thirty-First."

"I'm not taking your van."

"It's *armored*, Abe." I tried to smile. "How can you say no to an armored van?"

"Because it's had a lot of dead people in it."

"I haven't transported any corpses in...days," I said. "Look, you can give it to SWAT, or donate it to the Rescue Mission or something. Just take the keys, please." Part of the reason I wanted my van looked after was sentimental. It had been my home for years, and I didn't want it destroyed by the city.

Reluctantly, he scooped up the keys and ticket, and shoved them in a pocket. "Fine. But I'm only holding onto them because I don't want you losing your keys in some weird-ass fairy realm," he said. "Getting them back'd be a bitch."

"Thank you."

He sat silent another moment, and said, "Well, if you don't have any other bad news for me, guess you'd better get some rest for your...magic traveling, or whatever."

"I guess so," I said. "You too—now that you have to work normal-people hours."

"Yeah. I just love this promotion."

"Don't I know it," I said.

I walked him to the door, and he stopped before he went out. "You can do this, Gideon," he said. "Go save your family...and come back in one piece."

"Hey, I have to, right? Because not all my family's over there," I said. "The part I care about most is standing right here, telling me not to get my dumb ass killed."

He grabbed me, and I hugged him back hard. I felt his shoulders heave once, then he stepped back without looking at me. "Take care, kid," he said thickly. "And call me when you get back."

"I will."

When the door closed behind him, I leaned against the wall with my eyes shut.

It was a long time before I trusted my legs to get me back upstairs.

CHAPTER 13

It took me a minute to realize the weird buzzing sound was my phone. I only set the alarm when I had to get up at ungodly o'clock—and eight in the morning definitely qualified, for someone who often didn't even go to bed until now.

Once I'd gotten that straight, I had to puzzle out why there was something warm and solid pressed against me. And I finally figured it was Sadie.

I'd meant to sleep in the chair. Honest.

When I came back up from tearing my guts out with Abe, she'd been thrashing and moaning on the bed. Having a hell of a nightmare. I managed to half-wake her, and she muttered something about not wanting to be alone, and could I lay down with her until she fell asleep.

So I did. The next thing I knew, it was morning.

And I couldn't remember the last time I'd actually slept in a bed with another person.

Sadie stirred, and my brain registered that the alarm was still going off. I maneuvered carefully to sit on the edge of the bed, grabbed my phone from the nightstand beside it, and tapped it silent.

"Umph," Sadie slurred behind me. "'S morning now?"

I got up and paced a few steps away before I answered. Maybe we wouldn't talk about the whole bed-sharing thing. "Well, the sun's up," I said. "Probably." This room didn't have windows, but I was pretty sure sunrise came before eight.

"Good." Sadie straightened, pushed the covers down and ran a hand through unruly auburn curls—while I tried not to notice how absolutely adorable she was in the morning. "There a shower here?"

"Yeah, right there." I pointed to the small bathroom door. "You can use it first."

"I planned on it." She smiled sleepily and swung her legs off the bed. "Gideon...thank you. For staying with me."

I gave a slight cough. "No problem."

"Yes, it was. But you did it anyway."

Sure. It was a problem, in a you're-with-my-brother way. But now wasn't the time to bring that up. "Er, we should get ready," I said. "I have no idea when 'early' is supposed to be, but I'm guessing it's soon."

She sighed and stood. "You're right. I'll be quick," she said, brushing past me to head for the bathroom.

I probably should've said something else right there. Unfortunately, I had no idea what.

While she was in the shower, I double-checked the bags we'd brought up last night—Sadie's just to make sure it was still there. I had no idea what she'd packed. But I had a few changes of clothes, the spelled dagger Taeral gave me, and two of the guns we'd liberated from Milus Dei, with extra ammo. Didn't know what we'd face over there, but I figured a bunch of bullets would slow most things down.

As long as I could manage to hit them. I wasn't the world's best shot.

By 8:30, we were both showered and dressed. We left the room and found Cobalt and Will at the table in the small dining area, looking no more awake than either of us felt. But they'd put out quite a breakfast.

"That's a lot of food," I said, staring at a table full of bacon and sausage, buttered toast, breakfast pastries, two kinds of juice, and one of those fancy egg pies—couldn't remember what it was called. "How long have you been awake?"

Cobalt laughed under his breath. "Not that long. There's a diner nearby, and they deliver," he said. "Coffee's on the counter, if you'd like. Help yourselves."

"Thanks."

"I'll get us coffee." Sadie headed for the pot. She hadn't said much since we woke up, and apparently she didn't plan to.

I couldn't blame her. I'd never been on Death Row, but right now I could imagine what it felt like to sit down to the last meal.

———◆———

Uriskel turned up shortly after we stopped trying to eat—but I almost didn't recognize him.

Yesterday's leather and straps had been replaced by a rough, dark green sleeveless tunic over a full-sleeved black shirt, formfitting black pants, and simple suede boots. His dark red hair had somehow grown about a foot, and he'd acquired some fierce-looking facial tattoos. He carried a pack much bigger than ours on his back, and smaller bags in each hand.

There was something else, too. A bunch of feathers sticking up behind his shoulder, which I finally figured out were arrows to go with the bow fastened alongside the pack.

"A bow and arrow?" I said. Not even a round of bullets could kill a Fae, so a simpler weapon didn't make much sense. "Are they enchanted or something?"

Uriskel smiled crookedly and shook his head. "They're not for battle," he said. "We'll need to eat, and there's a shortage of things such as grocery stores and electricity in Arcadia."

"Oh. Right." I hadn't even thought about how different this place was going to be, other than full of Fae instead of humans. At least I knew how to hunt—but I wasn't exactly thrilled with the way I'd learned.

Cobalt looked him over and nodded approval. "It's been long since I've seen you this way, brother," he said. "Interesting markings. But you might've asked me, you know. I'd have done them better."

"It's only a glamour," Uriskel said. "I've shifted it a bit. Hoping we'll be mistaken for wild ones at a distance, and avoided for a time. Speaking of." He tossed one of the small bags at me, then walked over and handed the other one to Sadie. "Enter Arcadia dressed like that, and you'll be instant targets. I've more appropriate clothing for you."

Sadie shivered a little. With whispered thanks, she headed for the guest room.

"I'll just wait for her," I said, and opened the drawstring bag for a peek. Dark green and black stuff—probably an outfit similar to Uriskel's. "So, um. What wild ones?"

"The Unseelie of the wood," Uriskel said. "They're largely…unpleasant, and avoided by those more civilized, who don't find violence and mayhem quite as entertaining."

"Terrific."

It wasn't long before Sadie came out dressed in black and forest green. She looked amazing, but I couldn't bring myself to tell her that. Compliments seemed inappropriate for an outfit designed to help rescue the love of her life from certain death. So I just waved a little as I passed by on the way to the guest room.

I changed quickly, and then glanced in the bathroom mirror, figuring I probably looked like Peter Pan in this stuff. But I was surprised to find my reflection seemed a little more intimidating than a Disney cartoon. In fact, it was almost threatening.

Must've been subconscious. I was probably still thinking about the wild ones, and it'd rubbed off on my perceptions or something.

When I rejoined the rest of them, Sadie gaped at me. "Holy shit."

I frowned. "What?"

"Um. I've just never seen you look so…Fae before," she said.

Will smiled. "It suits you."

"Interesting," Uriskel said. "And now if we could all end the fashion discussion, we've places to go, and miles to make."

The silence that followed stretched into awkward territory, until Cobalt said, "Safe returns, then. All of you."

"That'd be the plan."

Uriskel moved to the center of the room, and Sadie and I followed. "I'll put us near to the Trees of Ankou as possible, though we'll still face a hike across the marshlands," he said. "The Mists tend to be active there. I can't risk stepping directly into them."

I frowned. "What Mists?"

"Let's hope you'll not have to find out." He raised a hand, paused, and then drew it down like a slow-motion karate chop.

The air rippled apart as his hand passed through, creating a slit that pulsed and gleamed with brilliant colors of every shade and hue—and some I couldn't even name. The gap almost seemed to breathe, a slow and slumbering pace that calmed my racing heart.

"All right. You first, DeathSpeaker. Then the girl," Uriskel said. "Don't wander off. I'll be directly behind you."

I nodded and moved in front of the rip. This wasn't the way I expected my first visit to Arcadia to happen—but I was going. No turning back now.

I stepped through before I could think myself out of it.

———◦●◦———

The first thing I noticed was the moon.

There'd been no bright lights or sudden darkness. No sense of time passing, no rush of air or weightless suspension. Going through the portal was like stepping from one room to the next—except the first room was completely gone, and the next one wasn't a room. It was a vast, wide open space under a brilliant and impossibly huge moon.

But it wasn't like any full moon I'd ever seen.

Pure blue steel, ringed by a shimmering corona like silver flames. The light eradicated every feature, erased the familiar shadows that textured the moon I knew. And there was something else off, something I only realized when I tore my gaze deliberately from the bright circle.

The sky was cloudless, velvet black with a faint purple hue.

And there were no stars. Not a single one.

A startled intake of breath behind me announced Sadie's arrival. I turned toward her—and the hesitant smile on my face froze as alarms blared through my head.

Full moon.

A full moon was very bad for a werewolf. And this was the fullest damned moon ever to exist.

All thoughts of taking in the surroundings vanished. "Sadie," I said carefully. "I think I figured out why you being here is not good."

She didn't seem to hear me. Her wide eyes saw the moon, and nothing else.

Just then, Uriskel stepped from the glowing gap in the air beside her. He gestured dismissively, and the jagged line of light vanished. "Well, at least that went smoothly."

"I'm not so sure about that," I rasped.

His brow furrowed, and he glanced at Sadie. Then he took a rapid step back. "Oh. Damn."

"Yeah."

Sadie shuddered violently. Her breath quickened, heaving in and out in rough gasps. "Gideon," she panted—and her eyes flashed wolf gold as she looked at me. "*Run.*"

CHAPTER 14

The wolf seemed to explode out of her.

I caught a brief flash of fur and fangs and claws, before Uriskel shoved me aside and threw an arm up. "*À dionadth!*"

Shield. I knew that one.

Sadie lunged at the exact time he spoke. She crashed into nothing, yelped and fell—but sprang right back up, fangs bared. A powerful swipe at the shield, and her claws sparked along the invisible barrier in a blue-white spray.

Okay, *that* didn't happen back in our realm.

With an almost human snarl of frustration, Sadie pivoted and walked slowly to the left and dragged her claws along the shield, showering sparks. Looking for the end point. Her eyes glittered redly, her lips lifted away from her fangs in a constant low growl.

Uriskel raised a hand to cast another spell.

"Wait!" Somehow I knew that whatever he threw next, it'd be a hell of a lot more damaging than a shield. I cut in front of him and gestured at Sadie. "*Beith na cohdal.*"

My pendant flashed a blinding white that nearly rivaled the moon.

And I remembered that the sleep spell hadn't worked on werewolf Sadie the last time I tried it.

But before I could panic properly, Sadie slowed almost to a complete stop. Her eyes dulled, and she took a single, staggering step. Then she slumped against the unseen shield and slid to the ground.

"Huh," Uriskel said with something like approval. "I'd not have thought of that."

"Yeah, well it's one of like three spells I know," I said, rushing around to Sadie's still form. "And it shouldn't have worked. It didn't before."

He flicked a gesture and stepped across where the shield had been. I couldn't help noticing how calm he was for someone who'd almost been mauled by a werewolf. "Presumably, you were in the human realm when you last attempted it," he said. "There's far more magic here, and your stone enhances the power."

"That wasn't exactly intentional," I said. "I have no idea why it did that."

Uriskel sighed. "You know even less than I suspected. I'd not thought that possible."

"Don't worry. I'm a fast learner." I crouched beside Sadie. Definitely unconscious...but still a werewolf. We couldn't just keep putting her to sleep the whole time we were here. "How long does your full moon last?" I said.

"In human terms, roughly two weeks."

"Great. What are we supposed to do with her?"

He shrugged. "Send her back."

"Not happening."

"What do you suggest, then?" he snapped. "Perhaps we should craft her a muzzle and leash, and drag her about the realm like a rabid dog."

"You're not helping." I rubbed my forehead, as if I could massage an answer from nothing. "There has to be something. A spell, a fancy glamour, something to...keep the light away from her," I finished slowly.

Something that would absorb it.

Like a stone that sucked up moonlight.

I grasped the cord around my neck, and hesitated. Not once in over a decade had I taken the pendant off. I'd promised to keep it safe, long before I knew that promises could be deadly to the Fae.

But it would be safe with Sadie. I had no doubt of that.

"What in blazes are you doing?" Uriskel said as I slipped the moonstone over my head.

"The stone absorbs moonlight to recharge." I lifted Sadie's heavy, furred head and eased the cord into place. "Maybe if she wears it, it'll draw enough light to keep her from going wolf."

He snorted. "Interesting. Perhaps you're not as thick as I believed."

"Gee, thanks."

I moved back a little and held my breath. The moonstone took on a milky glow—and a faint shadow washed over Sadie like dark, spreading water. Her fur and fangs started to retract.

Holy shit. It was actually working.

Then I remembered what would happen when she finished transforming, and stood between her and Uriskel. "How about you turn away for a minute?" I said.

"What are you...oh." A tiny smile graced his lips. "I've little interest in the female form," he said. "But if you insist."

He turned and walked a few steps away, and I thought of Cobalt saying *what am I supposed to tell Trystan?* The way Uriskel's voice broke when he said *I'll tell him myself.*

So Trystan was more than a relative. And I'd taken Uriskel away from him.

Just when I thought I couldn't feel like any more of an asshole.

Uriskel shrugged his pack off, opened it and removed a rolled blanket. He handed it back without looking. "For the moment," he said. "Once you wake her, we'll decide what to do about clothing her."

"Thank you," I said. "Listen, I'm sor—"

"Don't apologize to me. I'll not tolerate grousing."

For some reason, his gruff tone didn't make me as angry as it should've.

I shook the blanket loose and covered Sadie, then knelt next to her. "*Diúsaegh.*"

Her eyes opened. She gasped and clutched involuntarily at the blanket. "Oh, God," she whispered. "Did I…hurt anyone?"

"No. We're all fine."

"That moon. I've never felt anything like—" She jerked upright and stared in horror at the sky. "It's still up! Get away from me," she said, trying to scramble back. "I can't control it. Please…I don't want to hurt you."

"Whoa. You're okay." I smiled and pointed at the pendant. "Something to keep the wolf at bay."

She glanced down. "Your moonstone," she said hoarsely, touching the glowing gem with trembling fingers. "Gideon, I can't…are you sure?"

I nodded. "As long as we're here, it's yours."

"Thank you," she said. "I promise I'll keep it safe."

"I know you will."

Uriskel cleared his throat. "If you're through mooning at one another, perhaps you'd consider moving. We cannot stay in the open for long," he said. "Just dress in whatever you have. We're leagues from our destination yet, and we risk discovery the longer we remain still."

I managed not to snap at him—because unfortunately, he was probably right.

CHAPTER 15

I had to admit, Uriskel had a point about the clothes. Dressed in a normal human outfit, Sadie stood out in this place like a phone booth in ancient Greece.

At least her backpack hadn't been destroyed by the unexpected transformation, but both straps had broken. She'd tied them together and slung the bag across a shoulder without comment.

Despite the fast pace Uriskel set as we moved across the marshlands, I couldn't help gawking at everything. The moonlight should've washed out most colors, especially since it was so bright—but the landscape was starkly vibrant. At first the impossibility, the *wrongness* of the dark light made my head ache, but I got used to it gradually.

The terrain consisted of tufts, patches and long banks of grass in variegated greens, purples and reds, interspersed with sweeping curves and swells of black water that glinted blue with the moon. The occasional sketch of a lone, skeletal tree dotted the landscape, and an abrupt line of thick forest smudged the distant horizon. And some kind of shrub grew in thickets from stagnant pools of water—gnarled and twisting branches, glossy midnight-blue leaves shapes like teardrops, and dime-sized emerald green berries.

Ahead and to the right was a massive cluster of blue shrubs. A dark, shifting cloud of something hung over it. As we got closer, a low buzzing sound filled the air, like a swarm of bees—and I noticed small shapes detaching from the cloud and darting into the shrubs.

Uriskel sent an uneasy glance at the thicket and changed direction, heading sharply to the left.

Sadie and I rushed to catch up. "What is that?" I said.

"Sprites," he replied without looking back. "Feeding on thimbleberries."

"And sprites are...bad."

"Aye. You'll not want to go near them," he said. "A clutch of sprites can be deadly if they swarm."

Well, that sounded fun. "So they're insects?"

"More or less."

Just then, a small, dark shape zoomed past my face in the direction of the bushes. It moved too fast to make out, but I had the impression of an oversized wasp—plump, ungainly and menacing.

Sadie recoiled and swatted at the air in front of her. "What the hell...?"

Another shape zipped by the side of my head, drilling my ear with a whining buzz. Something heavy enough to be horrifying bumped into my arm—three quick, vibrating nudges, like a bee trying to fly through a closed window.

Then it darted up, circled twice and hovered less than a foot from my face.

"Uh. Uriskel." I froze, unable to take my eyes off the creature. Apparently a sprite was what happened when Tinkerbell and a four-inch hornet had a baby. The thing had a tiny, humanoid face with black oildrop eyes, a button nose, and a mouth full of bone-colored needles. Four arms with hands, two legs with feet. Two pairs of shimmering dragonfly wings. And a bulging thorax ending in a wickedly curved stinger.

It looked hungry.

From what seemed like a great distance away, I heard Uriskel say, "Kill it."

"But it's a...person. Sort of." I wasn't sure I could bring myself to murder a tiny, flying human-ish whatever. It was actually kind of cute, if you ignored the insectile ass end. And the teeth.

"It's an insect," he snarled. "Kill it, now."

"Jesus. All right. How?"

"Crush the damned thing! Quickly, before it—"

A high-pitched wail that sounded like Hell's teakettle burst from the sprite. It dove at me, and sunk its teeth-needles into my throat.

I gagged on a shout and stumbled back, brushing frantically at the thing. It refused to dislodge. Its thorax started to swell, and faintly glowing red liquid pulsed and swirled just beneath the leathery surface of the skin, stretching it like a balloon.

I grabbed the thing, shivering at the repulsive heat of it, and tried to yank it off me. Its teeth held fast.

Okay, it wasn't even kind of cute anymore. Screw it. I'd just swat it dead and pry the damned thing loose. I raised a hand, and registered Uriskel's shouted warning just as I brought it down hard and fast.

The sprite's distended thorax burst, spattering my throat with the glowing red liquid.

Which promptly started to sizzle and burn into my skin.

Suddenly Uriskel was there, forcing my head back while he poured water from a leather canteen down my neck. The sizzling stopped, and the screaming burn settled to a throb. He pried the remains of the world's freakiest bug out, dropping the tiny corpse indifferently to the ground, and then leaned in to inspect the damage. "You'll live," he pronounced gruffly.

"Oh, good." The rasping groan I managed to produce suggested that living would hurt for a while. "You okay, Sadie?"

"I hate bugs." She stood several feet away, her arms crossed in front of her like a shield. "I mean, I *really* hate bugs. What the hell kind of bug was that?"

"The kind that drinks your blood and turns it to acid, which it then injects you with," Uriskel said. "Unless you crush the blasted thing *before* it bites you."

I shuddered. "That stuff was my blood?"

"Aye. And if you'd like to keep it inside your body, you'll learn to kill sprites quickly."

"I think I got it."

"Good. Keep moving, then."

I decided I should probably listen to him from now on.

CHAPTER 16

We'd been walking for what felt like hours, but the scenery stayed the same. Colossal fiery moon, colorful grass and black water, blue bushes, clouds of sprites. None as big as the first one we'd passed, but as far as I was concerned, any number of those bloodsucking little bastards was too many.

The trees on the horizon looked no closer than they had when we started out.

Uriskel had the lead. Sadie was just behind him, and I brought up the rear of the column. We'd tried wandering along in the same general direction as him, but after drenching our feet with a half-dozen plunges into chilled water we hadn't seen, we both stayed in line with the guy who had dry boots.

Unfortunately, the damage had already been done. If we didn't get to this Ankou place soon, or at least stop for a break, our feet were going to pay dearly. Sadie was already hobbling a little—she'd lost her boots in the change, and had to replace them with a pair of canvas sneakers.

"So how many...leagues do we have to go?" I said.

"Many." Uriskel didn't break stride or look back.

"What's your idea of many? Five, ten? Five hundred?"

"As many as it takes to get there."

Sadie stopped so shortly, I almost ran into her. "That's it," she said. "I'm done walking."

Uriskel slowed to a halt. He turned to face her, his expression dark. "Perhaps you'd like to return to the human realm, then," he said. "Because there is much more walking to go."

"Why are we doing this, anyway?" she burst out. "Going to find some fairy who might be in some trees somewhere, who maybe knew a DeathSpeaker once, who could be able to help you figure out your abilities, possibly? This is insane! No offense, Gideon, but don't you think finding Taeral and Daoin is a little more important than unlocking the next DeathSpeaker level, or whatever the hell we're trying to do?"

Okay, that kind of hurt. It wasn't like I had much choice. "You know I do. But—"

"If we attempted to save them now, we'd all die," Uriskel said. "*That* is why we're doing this. And even at full strength, the three of us combined stand a slim chance against the Unseelie Guard, at best."

"Yeah," I muttered. "What he said."

I probably would've tried to put a little less all-is-lost in my explanation, though.

"But we don't even know what they're doing to them." Sadie's features worked desperately. "We have no idea why they took them. They could be dead already."

"They've not killed them," Uriskel said.

"How do you know that?" she practically screeched. "How could you possibly know the Unseelie Court's plans for someone you don't know anything about?"

"Because I know the Courts!" His lip curled in a sneer, and he made a visible effort to calm himself. "Gods save us from hysterical females," he murmured.

"What did you say?"

"You heard me." He gave her a challenging stare. "Perhaps we may all benefit from a brief rest," he said. "But if you cannot calm yourself enough to carry on, I will send you back. You're of no use to your Taeral in this state."

I was half convinced she'd yank the pendant off and go wolf on him. But she stared back at him for a minute, and then her rigid posture relaxed. "Fine. Where are we supposed to rest?"

He looked slowly around the flat, damp, endless marshlands. "Must be one around here somewhere," he said under his breath. "*Nochtaan.*"

Reveal. I was startled at how quickly I understood the word. I'd heard it before, even used it once or twice, but usually it took me a lot longer to remember or translate Fae.

Unfortunately, nothing seemed to be revealed.

"There." Uriskel headed to the right, toward what looked like just another patch of grass. But when we got closer, I realized it was more like moss—an oddly straight stretch about five feet wide that angled up like a ramp.

The moss covered part of a stone structure that looked like half a bridge, extending to the center of a winding black water stream, where it abruptly cut off. The stream was the biggest continuous body of water I'd seen out here, maybe ten feet from bank to bank. And the bridge itself looked ancient—bleached stone, pylons blackened with moisture, thick ropes of moss hanging from the edges like green cobwebs.

Uriskel led us onto the unfinished bridge and sat cross-legged on the cobbled stone surface, near the end of it. "We cannot stay long," he said. "This structure's not meant for the likes of us."

Sadie and I took seats with identical groans of relief. At least we'd be off our feet and semi-dry for a few minutes. "What is this?" I said.

"It's a *daugha.* A Brownie dock," he said.

That had my attention. "Dock, as in boats?" A relaxing boat ride sounded better than trudging through the swamps right about now.

"Aye, but you'd not get far with a Brownie boat." Uriskel smirked, as if he'd read my mind, and held his hands out three feet apart. "That's about the size of them," he said. "Brownies aren't much bigger than sprites."

"Oh," I said. "Do they have...teeth?"

He almost laughed. "They don't bite. They also don't like to be seen—but they'll make themselves known soon enough, if we linger here crowding their space."

"How will they do that?"

"Most likely, by shifting the dock and dumping us in the stream."

Great. Weren't there any nice creatures in fairy land?

Sadie peeled off a sopping shoe and wrung it over the side of the bridge, then did the same with the sock beneath. Her foot was wrinkled and pale, like she'd soaked in a tub for too long. She sighed and started rubbing it with both hands. "Wish I could just go wolf from the ankles down," she said. "Paws are a lot tougher than feet."

"Do you not have better shoes than those?" Uriskel said.

She glared at him. "No, I don't. I had no idea what to pack for Arcadia, all right?"

"Hopeless. The lot of you." He reached down and pulled his own boots off, then tossed them toward her. He didn't have socks under them. "Wear those," he said. "Much longer in yours, and you'll end up bleeding. I'll not carry you the rest of the way."

"Um." She frowned at his bare feet. "What are *you* going to wear?"

"I'll be fine. Never was one for footwear, anyway."

"Are you sure—"

"Just wear them."

"All right," she said softly. She picked one up and frowned, turning the boot slowly in her hands. "Er, I think they're a little too big."

"They're Fae boots," he said. "They'll adjust to your size when you put them on."

"Right." With an uncertain expression, she slid her foot into the boot. And it shrank around her until it was molded snugly into place.

Okay. That was pretty cool.

Sadie bit her lip. "Thank you, Uriskel," she said. "As soon as my shoes dry, I'll give them back."

He shrugged off the thanks and looked at me. "I suppose you're in a similar state."

"Nah, I'll make it," I said. "I've slogged through worse than this."

"Have you."

"Yeah. We do have swamps in the human realm, you know."

His brow lifted. "Oh, yes. I'd forgotten that Manhattan is famous for its swamps."

"I haven't always lived in Manhattan," I said, a little more forcefully than I'd meant. This was getting too close to the things I didn't talk about. Time to change the subject. "Look, do you have any idea how much longer it'll be until we get to the trees? Hours, days, what?"

He stared at me thoughtfully, and I figured he wouldn't answer with anything useful. Again. But finally, he said, "Hours. Perhaps two or three, if we continue at the same pace."

"Thanks."

I shifted and looked away, knowing my little outburst was unwarranted. But I couldn't help it.

My past was not up for discussion.

CHAPTER 17

The last time I hung out in a cave, it was to hide from my brothers so they wouldn't shoot me right away.

But this cave was no rock-strewn mountain crevice. We'd reached the Trees of Ankou—towering, leafless giants with silver-gray bark and elevated root systems. Most of the roots were as big around as a normal tree back home, and the spider-like sprawl of them formed hollows beneath the main trunks. The tree-cave we'd claimed was eight feet high, easy, and twice as long and wide. It was cool and dry, and the soft ground was fairly comfortable.

Which was probably a good thing, because it seemed like we'd be here longer than we wanted to.

"Anybody else get the idea this isn't working?" I said. With the eternal moon and all, I'd pretty much lost all sense of time. But I knew we'd been here thinking about our need to speak with Nyantha long enough for my boots to dry. So, multiple hours.

Sadie sat against one of the wide roots toward the back of the cave, hugging her knees to her chest. "I don't know, but I'm starving," she said.

"I suppose we should eat." Uriskel, who'd taken a post beside the only gap in the roots wide enough for us to squeeze into, looked through the opening into the murky light beyond. "It may be some time yet, though. I've not hunted these woods before, so I'm not familiar with the best areas to find game."

Oh, good. Hunting. I sighed and got up from the ground, hoping maybe it wouldn't be so bad now. At least I didn't have anyone waiting to beat me down for the slightest mistake—though I assumed Uriskel would have plenty of sarcastic remarks. "All right," I said. "What are we hunting?"

"*You* are hunting nothing," Uriskel said as he separated the bow and arrows from his pack. "Stay here. I'll return as soon as possible."

"Bullshit. I'm going with you."

"No, you are not." He stared coldly at me. "You know nothing of this place, its creatures, or the terrain. You'll only get in my way."

Okay, this you're-an-idiot attitude was really starting to bother me. "You're right. I don't know a damned thing about Arcadia," I said. "But I know hunting. If it's an animal, I can track it, bait it, flush it—everything but take it down, because I'm a lousy shot. So I hope you're not."

He subjected me to one of those long, appraising looks. At last he said, "Fine. But you'd best keep up, because I'll not restrain myself to your pace."

"Oh, I'll keep up." I heaved a breath and approached Sadie. Her mood had declined steadily while we trudged through the swamps, and she'd been mostly distant and detached for a while now. I was worried she'd already given up hope. "Hey," I said quietly, and waited until she looked at me. "Would you mind waiting here, in case this Nyantha person shows up?"

"Whatever," she murmured. "Just bring food."

I thought about trying to reassure her that we'd get them back, but that would probably make it worse. Besides, it was hard to sound convincing when I didn't quite believe it myself. "We'll find something," I said. "Be back soon."

She nodded and rested her head on her knees.

Trying to ignore the tight feeling in my chest, I went back to Uriskel. "So, let me ask again," I said. "What are we hunting?"

"The *fián'tormihr.*" He flashed an unpleasant smile. "They're similar to your wild boar, I suppose. Though they are larger and stronger, with more tusks, a bone-plated head, and poisoned bristles. Quite the badly-tempered, lethal beast."

"Great. Is there anything in Arcadia that won't try to kill us?"

"You're probably safe from the trees," he said. "Come on, then. Let's hunt."

If it wasn't this or starve, I might've changed my mind about going with him.

———————◆———————

Once I got past the strange light and the sheer size of things around here, it was easy enough to track. It just wasn't all that comforting. Regular wild boars were big and mean enough…but the signs confirmed this whatever-it-was would prove worse.

Maybe we could pick off a little sick one or something.

"And this is what, now?" Uriskel said. He'd fallen in behind me with a sort of reserved amusement, like he was just waiting to rub it in when this turned out to be a wild goose chase. But I'd already spotted quite a few signs of activity. It made sense that a boar-like creature would live in this area— swampy atmosphere, dense ground cover, plenty of vegetation. A wilderness that was rarely disturbed.

Just the kind of place I'd spent half my life praying to escape.

I gestured at the wide swath of packed ground we were following. "Highway trail," I said. "Boars tend to use the same main path. It'll branch off here and there, lead to rooting spots or hog wallows. That's where we'll find them."

"And you can locate these…branches."

"Yeah, I can." Matter of fact, it looked like there was one just ahead. I slowed and veered to the left, crouching at the base of a tree with several gashes in the trunk, three to four feet from the ground. "Tusk marks," I said, patting the gashes as I fished a loose stick out of the nearby underbrush. "And this is scat."

Damned big scat, I added silently, and poked the stick at the dark brown, fist-sized lumps on the ground. They crumbled

99

apart, revealing small bones, bits of fur, and clumps of disturbingly human-looking hair compacted into the waste.

I didn't want to know what—or who—the hair had belonged to.

"It's fresh," I said. "This way."

Uriskel raised an eyebrow, but he followed me without a word.

The smaller path grew progressively muddier, the ground to either side churned or flat-out torn up in some spots. Definitely rooting activity. In firmer places, I spotted the occasional cloven hoof print, half again as big as the biggest I'd seen before.

If we caught the thing, at least we'd have plenty of meat.

It wasn't long before the path emptied ahead into a sizeable clearing. I stopped just before the open area and held a hand up, telling Uriskel to wait. Then I crept closer and looked around. There was a large, round depression in the damp ground to the right, ringed with displaced dirt—a hog wallow. A few smaller trees near the wallow were smooth and caked with mud around the lower three feet or so, where the animal had frequently rubbed its tusks.

Toward the back of the clearing, something rustled softly in the underbrush. I stared at the spot until I made out glimpses of ivory between the dulled brown tangles. Then I could follow the vague shape of the thing humped in the weeds and probably watching us just as carefully.

It was distressingly big.

"There," I whispered. "You see it?"

Uriskel looked. His eyes widened the smallest bit. "Aye," he said in a low voice, and cocked his head slightly. "You've a plan to draw it out, then?"

"More or less." This'd never been my favorite part of the "family" hunt. They wouldn't let me touch the guns, or anything that resembled a weapon—but they sure as hell didn't hesitate to use me as bait. "I'll get it to charge me, and you stay out of sight and kill it," I said. "Er. How fast do you think you can take it out?"

"The hide of the *fián'tormihr* is quite thick," he said. "Likely, I'll need at least two clean shots to fell the beast. Perhaps three."

I sighed. "Terrific. Well, whenever you're ready."

"Are you not afraid?"

"Nah, not really. Just...resigned," I said. "Animals don't scare me. People do."

A strange expression came over his face. "Very well." He loosened his bow from his back and faded into the cover alongside the path. "Ready when you are," he called softly.

I nodded, let out a breath, and walked into the clearing.

For the most part, wild boars had no interest in people. If there was one around, they'd try to stay hidden as long as possible, until the person was practically on top of them. They'd only charge if you crowded their space.

But apparently this one considered the entire clearing its space—because I hadn't gotten halfway across before a living, breathing nightmare burst from the underbrush with a screeching roar.

It was four-legged and vaguely boar-shaped. That was where the resemblance ended. Glittering, red-shot gray eyes honed in on me from a face caged in four massive tusks, below a bony shield like a triceratops that crested its lowered head. Mud-streaked, mottled purple skin, spiny bristles fringed along its spine, and a thick cord of a tail that was more rat than hog, tipped with a cluster of curved spikes.

Don't move, you little bastard. I could practically hear Orville Valentine's barked commands, the first time they'd shoved me out to flush a wild hog. *You wait until the last second, so the sumbitch keeps runnin' once it passes you. Or tramples your weak ass—I don't much care which.*

Boar baiting was a lot like being a matador. Let it charge, sidestep, repeat until the animal got tired and gave up. Or in my case, until someone finally bothered to shoot it when they got bored with watching me scramble desperately out of the way.

101

At least Uriskel wouldn't wait that long. I hoped.

Somehow I managed to hold my ground until the monstrous thing was one leap from goring me. I dove aside, heard the high whine of an arrow. The beast squealed thunder.

When I got up, it was already charging again.

I let it come longer. This time it was running parallel to the tree line instead of head-on, so it should afford Uriskel a more damaging shot. At least he'd hit it the first time—the feathered shaft of the arrow protruded from the creature's left shoulder.

Two more mosquito whines sounded in rapid succession over the thunder of hooves. I jumped aside, felt the hot breath of the beast as it passed inches from me. And watched its barbed tail whip around and head straight for my face.

That was probably where the poison was.

Without thinking, I raised an arm to block it. *"Lahm à dionadth!"*

I didn't even realize I'd spoken the words, until the tail clanged against shimmering nothing in front of my arm and bounced off.

Holy hell. I'd actually remembered a spell when I needed it.

The beast galloped a few more feet full-steam before it stumbled and let out a bellowing roar. Then it toppled to the ground, panting and heaving, with fresh arrows sprouting from its side.

Uriskel burst from the tree line, bow at the ready, and sent an arrow neatly through its throat. The creature shuddered and stilled.

He turned to me with something that mostly resembled a smile. "Well done, DeathSpeaker."

"Yeah, you too," I said. "But do me a favor."

"What's that?"

"Call me Gideon. I'm not all that thrilled with the title, you know?"

He nodded. "All right…Gideon."

"Thanks."

It was strange. Uriskel seemed almost friendly, and for some reason I felt like I'd just passed some kind of test.

I only wished I knew what he'd been testing me for.

CHAPTER 18

Roasted *fián'tormihr* did not taste like chicken. It was greasy and a little gamey, like most wild meat, but surprisingly tender. Somewhere between pork and buffalo—which I'd actually had a few times.

The bulky carcass never would've fit through the entrance to the tree-cave, so we'd temporarily moved the party outside. With decent portions eaten and the rest of the beast cooking over a hastily dug pit fire, we sat on the ground in a loose semi-cirle near the base of the tree, awkwardly not speaking.

At least until I remembered I'd left out something important. In all the confusion and exhaustion of getting here, dealing with an unfamiliar world and the tension of facing damned near impossible odds for success, I'd forgotten to mention Reun.

"Uriskel...there's something I should probably tell you," I said.

He gave me a dry look. "I don't suppose it's good news."

"Not exactly." I coughed and stared at the fire. "Uh, we may be trying to rescue three people," I said. "After they took Daoin and Taeral, a friend of ours decided he had to save them on his own. He crossed over before we could stop him."

Uriskel frowned and rubbed a temple. "So this friend is Fae."

"Yeah. His name's Reun," I said. "I guess he's a Seelie noble, and—"

"*Reun?*" he cut in. "By the gods, you've a strange definition of friend."

"So you know him, too." I probably shouldn't have been surprised. He seemed to know all the important Fae, on both sides of the line. Which didn't make a lot of sense. The Seelie and Unseelie despised each other, but Uriskel wasn't taking sides. Apparently he just hated them all, with the exception of his brother.

It finally occurred to me that if Cobalt was a prince, and really his brother—then Uriskel must be, too.

And I had to wonder why he didn't mention that.

Sadie roused herself from staring dully at nothing, long enough to shoot him a narrow-eyed glance. "What's your problem with Reun?" she said. "I thought you'd be okay with him, at least. Taeral said you only hated your own kind."

"Sadie, don't," I whispered sharply. He'd finally settled down to semi-decent, and she was going to piss him off all over again.

He did look furious. But it only lasted for a few seconds, and then his jaw firmed and he looked away. "My own kind," he said hoarsely. "I'd likely despise them as well, if there were any of them."

"What are you talking about?" Sadie said. "You're Unseelie."

"I am. And yet, I am not." He closed his eyes briefly, and opened them frowning. "My mother was Unseelie. *Is* Unseelie, I suppose," he said reluctantly. "But my father..."

"Jesus Christ." I got it without him having to say another word. "Your father is Cobalt's father. The Seelie King."

He winced. "Aye, that's right. I am a halfling, the child of a forbidden union," he said. "And I should not have lived."

Sadie looked as shocked as I felt. "What do you mean, you shouldn't have lived?"

"As I said, it is forbidden." Uriskel clenched a fist, still refusing to look at either of us. "Halflings are summarily murdered at birth. But I was spared, because of my *royalty*." He spat the word like a curse. "And because the Seelie King had plans for me. When I came of age, I was made a ward of

105

the Summer Court. Essentially, their property. The perfect spy, able to pass as Unseelie and strike at their enemies."

The sadistic pet of the Seelie nobles. That's what Taeral had called him—and Uriskel hadn't denied it. "So you didn't have a choice," I said. "All that stuff about being a traitor, turning over your own kind..."

He nodded slowly. "I've done unspeakable things in the name of the Seelie Court. For two hundred years and more, I served their savage whims," he said. "Resistance or disobedience brought pain and suffering, and failure would've been my death sentence. Yet I'd have gladly died, were it not for the threat against my brothers."

"Brothers?" Sadie echoed. "As in, more than one?"

"Aye. There is Cobalt...and there is Braelan. The true Prince." He flashed a bitter smile. "The Seelie King forbid everyone who knew from telling Braelan of my true heritage. If he'd not discovered it on his own, I'd yet be a slave to the Court. But he and Cobalt conspired to set me free—and now Braelan is King."

Damn. I wasn't exactly happy that I'd been right when I thought Uriskel had been abused. But Jesus, for two hundred *years*? No wonder the guy had anger management issues. "I'm sorry, man," I said. "There are no words. But I have to say, I don't blame you for not explaining all this. Even when Taeral came after you the way he did."

He shrugged. "Cobalt tells me I should break my silence, inform everyone that I've done nothing wrong. He believes that, of course—that I am innocent. But I *have* done things. Terrible things. Coerced or not, they were still my actions," he said. "I am not as blameless as my brother believes. And so, I hold myself accountable...to ensure that it never happens again."

Did I ever understand that. He and I had a lot more in common than I thought. It hadn't been a week yet since I murdered a bunch of people to save another bunch, and telling myself they were the bad guys didn't help. Neither did being under the influence of Milus Dei's drug—because I'd taken it willingly. I injected myself.

No one would blame me for it, so I had to. Because I wasn't ever doing that again.

"Oh my God."

Sadie's frantic whisper drew my attention. I thought she just felt bad for Uriskel, but she wasn't looking at him. She was staring past me, her eyes wide and unblinking.

I wasn't sure I wanted to see whatever it was. But suddenly, I didn't have a choice—because "it" appeared between me and the fire pit. And it wasn't alone.

We were surrounded by ghosts.

CHAPTER 19

There were five of them. Semi-transparent women in hooded green robes with long, tangled hair, floating a few feet above the ground. Ancient, wrinkled faces, gleaming white eyes. Their robes shivered and flapped in the still air, as if a phantom wind blew only on them.

"Banshees," Uriskel grated before I could ask what the hell they were. "Do not engage them."

The one in front of me floated closer, holding her arms out wide. "Who calls upon Nyantha the wise, daughter of the spirits and guardian of the Trees of Ankou?" Her voice boomed out like a cannon, and the rolling echo of the words lingered in my ears.

I shuddered. Do not engage—yeah, right. They really looked like they were going to engage us, like it or not.

The banshee sighed, lowered her arms and planted a hand on her ghostly hip. "Well?" she said in a normal voice. "It *was* you lot calling, wasn't it?"

"Um." I blinked and glanced at Uriskel, who was busy staring open-mouthed at the banshee. "Yes?" I said.

"Well, ye can bloody well stop now, can't ye? Oberon's knees, we've been hearing the racket all morning."

This was not what I expected when I thought banshee. But I'd never actually met one, so maybe this was normal. "So...are you Nyantha?" I said.

The other banshees giggled, but they stopped with a stern look from the apparent leader. "Do I look Sluagh to ye, DeathSpeaker?"

I gave a slight frown. "You know who I am."

"Course I do. I'm dead, ain't I?"

I didn't know what to say to that.

Uriskel stepped forward with a wicked sneer. "What business is it of yours whether we speak with Nyantha, hag?"

"Hag! I'll have ye—"

One of the other banshees floated over to her, and I realized with a start that her face was smooth and unlined now. She whispered something in the leader's ear.

The lead banshee groaned. "Hang this bloody tradition," she muttered, rolling her eyes. "Nyantha the wise, indeed." She passed a hand down her face, and the old woman became young and breathtaking. Except for the creepy white eyes, and the whole being a ghost thing. "That better, then?" she said.

Uriskel was unmoved. "You still haven't answered my question. Banshee. Meddling is not in your job description."

"Typical," the banshee snorted. "Ye think it's all wailing and keening, washing bloody clothes at the river, that sort of shite? We get a noble death—what, every few hundred years, if we're lucky. And we're not just going to sit around meanwhile waiting for some nob to kick off, are we? Surely ye know this, *Prince* Uriskel."

"Enough," he snarled.

"Not one for labels, are ye?" she said with a smile. "Well, neither are we. So I'll kindly thank ye to stuff yer assumptions."

"All right," he said. "Point taken."

Sadie touched my arm, and I almost jumped. "What the hell's going on?" she said under her breath.

"I have no idea."

The leader managed to look offended. "Ye called for Nyantha," she said, like she was explaining to a distracted child. "We've come to take ye to her."

"About time." Uriskel said. "Give us a moment to pack, and—"

"Not you lot." The banshee's features looked almost apologetic as she pointed at me. "Only the one who seeks her counsel may enter the realm of the guardian."

Uriskel folded his arms. "The realm of the guardian. Really."

"Sorry. I don't make the rules," she said.

"And what promise do we have that you'll bring him back?"

The banshee bobbed up and down a few times. "I suppose ye shouldn't be left here alone, at any rate," she said. "All the trampling about ye've done since ye got here, psychically speaking, it's lucky ye didn't rouse something worse than us." She looked over her shoulder. "Pohn. Pehn."

Two of the other banshees floated over.

"My sisters'll stay with ye, until we've come back with yer friend," she said. "Will that do ye?"

"Fine," Uriskel grumbled.

Pohn and Pehn looked at each other, and then smiled teasingly at him. He rolled his eyes and turned away.

Well. This could get awkward.

"Are you all sisters?" I said, hoping to steer things in a different direction.

"All banshees are sisters, in a manner of speaking," the lead banshee said. "I'm Pan, by the bye. That's Pyn, and she's..." She waved a hand at the one who'd whispered in her ear. "Alice," she sighed dramatically.

Alice giggled and vanished abruptly, only to reappear at Pan's side, waggling her fingers at me.

"Okay," I said slowly. "I'm Gideon, and this is Sadie. I guess you know Uriskel."

"Right, then," Pan said. "Now we're all introduced, so let's go."

Sadie frowned and looked at me. "Are you sure about this?"

"No. But I promise I'll be back."

She nodded. "Hurry."

I definitely intended to try.

CHAPTER 20

It wasn't long before I lost all sense of direction in the unchanging forest.

Pyn floated in the lead, her hands pressed together solemnly in front of her. Pan stayed to my left, and Alice was apparently supposed to flank me on the right. But she kept vanishing in silky clouds of multi-colored smoke, or sinking slowly into the ground with an expression of mock horror, or air-swimming circles around the group.

She disappeared again, and then popped into view right in front of me. Upside down.

"Alice!" Pan hissed. "Can't ye stop fidgeting for five minutes?"

With a high-pitched giggle, Alice flipped in midair and landed on my right. She made a show of craning forward to look at Pyn, and then copied her sister's choir-girl posture and tried to look serious. But the corners of her mouth kept twitching.

I gave it two minutes. Three at the most.

Pan shook her head. "Ye'll have to forgive Alice," she said. "She's not been dead long, and the novelty hasn't worn off yet."

"Oh. Right." I guessed it was good to know there was novelty in being dead. But there was something else bothering me, and I'd finally figured out what it was. "Can I ask you something...Pan?" I said.

"Aye. As if I could stop ye, DeathSpeaker."

"Yeah, it's about that." I wasn't quite sure how to ask it. "You're dead, right?"

"Told ye that already, didn't I?"

"You did mention it. So...why aren't you afraid of me?"

"Should I be?" she said.

"Er, no. But all the other dead people have been, so far." I frowned. "And you keep answering my questions with questions. I didn't think you could do that."

"Well, I'd answer with answers, if ye'd ask me something that *has* an answer."

"Okay," I said. "Now I'm really confused."

She laughed, but there was nothing mocking in it. "Ye've no idea what it means to be the DeathSpeaker, do ye?" she said. "Just as green as our Alice, here."

Alice joined in with a giggle.

"You're right. I'm clueless," I said. "That's why I want to talk to Nyantha. I heard she knew the DeathSpeaker before me, and I was hoping she could help me figure all this stuff out."

"Oh, for the love of Titania. Ye'll swell her dear old head right up, and she'll be intolerably full of herself for weeks." Pan flashed a fond smile. "To answer the question, I don't fear ye because I'm already on the living side of the barrier—and I've no secrets to keep. Ye'll not understand that quite yet. But ye will, soon."

Oh, good. I could hardly wait.

———————◆———————

The realm of the guardian was a treehouse.

In defense of its mystical-sounding name, though, it was a hell of a treehouse. The structure spanned a group of three trees, with hanging wooden bridges connecting buildings so high up, they looked like ornate birdhouses. A light mist swirled the air above the mini-compound, glinting blue in the blazing moonlight.

113

The banshees led me up a spiral staircase that seemed to be carved into one of the trees—the one supporting the largest house. When we reached the top, Pyn and Alice disappeared.

"Where'd they go?" I said.

"Oh, they're just following the rules. Realm of the guardian, only one may enter, et cetera and so forth." Pan smiled crookedly and gestured at the arched wooden door in front of us. "Ye'll have to open that," she said. "What with my being incorporeal."

"Got it." I grabbed the tarnished brass doorknob, turned it, and pushed the door open.

Inside was a living room with a green carpet, wooden walls, and off-white furniture. At least, that's what my brain saw at first. I gradually realized that the walls were living branches, the floor was a carpet of moss—and the furniture was made out of bones.

Okay. That was a little unsettling.

"Nyantha," Pan called as she drifted past me into the center of the room. "Ye've a visitor here. Isn't that exciting?"

There was a throat-clearing sound from a shadowed doorway on the other side of the room.

Pan slumped and let out a long-suffering sigh. "Presenting Nyantha the wise, daughter of the spirits and guardian of the Trees-of-Ankou-come-seeker-of-knowledge-and-speak-your-questions-forthwith."

Another deliberate cough.

"Really, Nyantha," she muttered, extending her arms wide. She threw her head back, and light poured from her white eyes, filling the room with blinding light.

When it faded, Pan was gone, and someone else stood in her place.

Nyantha was surprisingly tall. Long, straight white hair fell to her waist, and her eyes were the purple of a twilight sky. Not a single line, crease or wrinkle marked her elegant face, but she still seemed ancient, timeless. She wore a simple black, shimmering gown and silver rings on every finger, and on every toe of her bare feet.

She smiled. "You know my grand-niece. What a delight," she said. "How is Shade?"

"I think she's fine, ma'am," I stammered, trying to remember if I'd actually said that.

"Such lovely manners." The Sluagh seemed to drift when she walked. Her feet barely whispered on the moss beneath them. "Welcome, DeathSpeaker. How can I help you?"

I had no idea where to start. I wanted to know about the barrier Pan had mentioned, and why it hurt when I spoke to the dead. Why sometimes I had to physically touch the corpse to contact them, and other times they just started talking to me. Why I couldn't do it for very long, and what made me pass out when I did. Whether there was anything else I could do besides force dead people to speak.

"I see." Nyantha smiled again. "You'd like to know everything."

I got over the surprise pretty fast. "Right. You're psychic," I said. Couldn't help wondering if it worked the same as Shade's abilities, if she'd only hear what I wanted her to. Or if she could read anything she wanted in my head.

Nyantha raised an eyebrow. "I can read anything," she said. "But I'll try to stay away from your dark secrets, Gideon Black."

This time I was a bit unnerved. "I'd appreciate that."

"I know." She winked and held a hand out. "Shall we, then?"

"Okay," I said hesitantly.

I took her hand, and the world went away in a dizzying swoop of weightlessness.

And then we were in a cemetery.

CHAPTER 21

"It's quite simple, really. You merely decide to be somewhere else."

"How did you do that?" I blurted, before my mind processed that she'd already answered the question I hadn't asked. "Um, right. Simple." It didn't sound simple to me. I decided I wanted to be somewhere else all the time, but I'd never suddenly found myself there. Of course, *anywhere but being shot at by bad guys* wasn't a very specific destination.

Daoin had done something like that. Once, and probably by accident.

"You are the child of Lord Daoin?" Nyantha said. "How is he...oh. Oh, my."

"Yeah. That." I must've thought about Daoin and Taeral, and Reun, and why we'd come here unprepared and desperate instead of the way Taeral planned. Sadie had told me to hurry, but I didn't need the prompt. I knew the longer this took, the more they'd suffer. And maybe we were too late. Despite Uriskel's assurances, I couldn't help thinking that if the Unseelie Court wanted them dead—they would be.

Nyantha smiled sadly. "They live yet," she said. "Moirehna has no intention of destroying them. She seeks revenge, for a heart she believes broken."

I stared at her. It wasn't easy getting used to this psychic stuff.

"The Unseelie Queen," she said as I opened my mouth to ask *who's Moirehna.* "And yes, I'll try to wait until you ask a question."

Damn. I hadn't even thought that far ahead. The question didn't form in my mind until after she'd answered—and I had to force myself not to say it out loud anyway.

"Thanks," I said. At least that was in the right place.

It'd take a few minutes for my head to stop spinning, from trying to follow a conversation that somehow happened before I had it. So I leaned on a nearby gravestone to catch my breath and look around.

Grass covered the grounds here, like the marshlands—but it was glossy black. A low-lying blue mist, like the stuff above Nyantha's treehouse, drifted around and between the thick, inky stalks, occasionally splashing against a stone and billowing up the surface until it poured down the other side like ghostly water.

The grave markers themselves weren't uniform, and there were few that resembled traditional headstones. Some were obelisks, like the one I'd leaned against. Others were cairns, or boulders, or rough stone sculptures. They were marked with runes instead of names, and they didn't seem to be arranged in any particular pattern. No rows or columns or grids.

Or so I thought, until I spotted the tower of black stones in the center of the place and realized the graves formed a widening spiral from there.

"Okay," I finally said, hoping to start a normal conversation this time. "Shade says you knew the guy who was the DeathSpeaker before me, right?"

Nyantha nodded. "I did. Poor, mad Kelwyyn," she said.

"Er. Mad Kelwyyn?"

"Yes, he was. Eventually." She sighed and folded her hands together. "He'd learned to kill with a word, you see. One word that could rip the very soul from you and destroy it forever—a feat only the DeathSpeaker can accomplish. He'd used it just once, to stop a power-hungry sorcerer with designs to enslave all of Arcadia. But the High Fae decided that Kelwyyn himself was too powerful…and so, to keep him in line, they murdered his daughter."

117

"Jesus Christ." Somehow I didn't see pissing off someone more powerful than you as being an effective way to stop them.

"Indeed, it was not," Nyantha said, and I ignored the fact that I hadn't said that out loud. "His grief drove him to slaughter anyone who came near him. The more he killed, the harder they tried to destroy him. But they could not touch him. Their final attempt, thirty of the oldest and strongest nobles armed with lethal weapons and spells, lasted less than half a day against him."

"Wait. I thought they killed him," I said. "He's still alive?"

"Perhaps...but no one will ever know for certain. In the end he removed himself, the only way he could." She looked off to the distance. "The Fae are not capable of taking their own lives," she said. "And so, Kelwyyn walked into the Mists."

Uriskel had mentioned those, too. "What are the Mists?"

"Agents of change," she said. "The Mists...take things, and sometimes leave other things in their place."

I frowned. "What kind of things?"

"Cottages, fields, ponds. Forests and villages. Once, an entire realm. Those sorts of things—sometimes along with the living creatures they contain." She looked at me, and added, "No one knows what happens inside them, because nothing alive has ever returned from the Mists."

"Great." So being the DeathSpeaker meant I'd eventually go crazy, kill a bunch of people, and wander off to vanish into who-knows-what forever.

"Not necessarily," Nyantha said. "All right, then, DeathSpeaker. Let me show you how to speak to the dead properly."

That was definitely going to be my next question.

———◆———

The marker she led me to was a cairn of stones, carefully placed to form a flat-topped pyramid about four feet high. There was a large, flat stone with carved runes embedded in the top of the cairn.

She didn't mention who was buried there.

"The barrier between the land of the living and the world of the dead exists all around us." Nyantha took a seat on a stone bench alongside the grave. "You've the ability to reach through that barrier, and pull souls through to the living side."

"Is that what I'm doing?" I said, vaguely horrified.

"Yes, but the souls take no harm in visiting this side. Many do so voluntarily. My banshees, for example," she said. "The remains of the dead serve as a kind of touchstone, an anchor to the living realm. In a sense, they are always connected to their remains, no matter where they roam. That is why you can reach them when you're near a body."

I nodded, trying not to think too hard about the world of the dead. "So that's why it's easier when I touch them?"

"That's right. But you do not need physical contact with the remains to compel a soul. It simply helps you to focus your efforts." She smiled. "With practice, you'll be able to call on them without touch."

"Practice. Terrific."

Her brow furrowed. "You are concerned about the pain," she said. "The act of crossing the barrier is painful, and always will be—for you, and the soul. But once you've brought them over, you can speak to them without damaging yourself or the dead."

"Yeah, that's what I'm hoping," I said. "I just don't know how to do it."

"You must release the soul." She pointed at my head. "The reason for the pain, the bleeding, is that you hold them in your mind. And you've no room in there for more than one. Every word, every movement of the soul tears at you...and the soul is constantly crushed, causing them pain as well."

I felt a little sick, knowing I'd done that to people's souls. Most of them were bad guys—but not all of them had been. "So how do I release them?"

"Kelwynn always projected them outward, like a glamour," she said. "But be cautious. You must hold part of them back, because if you lose your grip, a determined soul may escape

119

back to the world of the dead—or worse, free itself to the realm of the living."

Oh, good. Another whole new way for me to screw things up.

"Have confidence in your abilities, DeathSpeaker." She nodded at the cairn, and said, "Go on, then. Give it a try."

"What, now?"

"Yes, now. You cannot improve your abilities merely by talking about them."

I frowned at the marker. "Who's buried here, anyway?"

She cleared her throat with flair. "Here lies a great challenge, and a fitting test for your powers. The most stubborn, uncooperative, exasperating Fae in all the realms," she said. "My sister."

"Your sister," I repeated. "Let me guess. She lied to you about something, and you want me to make her tell the truth."

A shocked expression formed on her face. "I simply know she'll fight you, and wanted to ensure you'd have a true test," she said—and then flashed a sly smile. "But yes. The lying part is important as well. Consider it payment for my wise advice."

"I can do that," I said with a grin. "Well…here goes."

At first I wasn't sure how to start. Having a handy corpse was definitely easier, but there was six feet of grass and dirt between me and this one. So I reasoned that I was standing on the ground, and the ground was on her. Technically, I was in contact.

"Hey. Nyantha's sister," I murmured. "We need to talk."

There was a tug in my head. Just once, and then it was gone.

"Damn. Hold on." I closed my eyes and focused on the ground beneath me, the body that was down there somewhere.

And I felt something run through me. A surge of energy that stretched down like a rubber band, into the dirt. I could sense the cool dampness of it.

Then I swore my fingers brushed smooth, solid bone. Which I was nowhere near.

The rubber-band energy snapped back into me. There was a wave of pain, and the tugging started in earnest. *Let go of me, DeathSpeaker!* a female voice shrieked in my head. *I swear, if Nyantha has something to do with this, I'll...I'll melt your brain!*

I smirked in spite of the pounding. "Pretty sure you can't do that," I said.

I am a powerful psychic. Release me at once!

"If you say so." I glanced at Nyantha. "Well, she's in there," I said. It kind of weirded me out, knowing there was an actual soul banging around in my head. "Now what?"

"Now you simply project her into the world."

"Uh-huh," I said. "Does this part come with step-by-step instructions?"

"I'm afraid not."

"Okay, then. Guess I'll wing it."

I tried for a few minutes. It wasn't easy to concentrate, with her struggling and shouting in Fae that I half understood. Once I was pretty sure she called me a worm's disease-ridden asshole, or something close to that. But even when I managed to focus, nothing happened.

Maybe I needed a prop. I could project glamour onto someone else—I'd done it to Sadie out of desperation, when I was trying to break her out of Milus Dei headquarters in New York. I didn't want to turn Nyantha into her sister. But I could try using an object.

The cairn was the closest substantial thing. I turned to face it and thought hard: *You are Nyantha's sister.*

I felt like a complete idiot. But the pile of stones started to change.

As the shape formed, Nyantha stood from the bench and drifted to my side, watching intently. Soon I had a blurry, person-shaped blob that gradually resolved into a woman. Long white hair like her sister's, pale blue eyes, dressed in a white gown. And semi-transparent, enough to see the landscape behind her.

She did not look happy.

After I got over staring at her, I finally realized the pain had left my head. There was still a faint sense of pressure, like an invisible string drawn taut between me and the ghost-woman. But it didn't hurt.

"Good," Nyantha whispered. "That means you've still got hold of her. Do not let go."

"*Nyantha.*" The hollow, almost buzzing voice was outside my head, and I didn't feel it at all. "*I knew this was your doing. So this is the new DeathSpeaker, is he? An Unseelie halfling with human blood.*"

She shouldn't have known that. "Aren't you dead?"

"*Obviously. But I am still psychic.*" An unsettling smile flickered across her transluscent face. "*Your mind is not a pleasant place...Gideon.*"

"Yeah, no shit." I glowered at her. "What's your name?" I said, more out of habit than any desire to find out. It was the first question I always asked dead people—if they didn't already know that they couldn't lie to me, that was usually when they figured it out.

"*Dyandrea. But my dear sister could have told you that.*" Her pale eyes sizzled with irritation. "*What do you want, as if I don't already know?*"

"Where is it, you greedy witch?" Nyantha said.

Dyandrea laughed. "*Why, sister. I've no idea what you mean.*"

"Yes, you do. My frost crystal."

"*What frost crystal?*"

"You see?" Nyantha gestured sharply at the spirit. "She's absolutely horrid, even when she's dead. Ask her where it is."

"*And she's completely starkers. Always has been.*"

"Stubborn lunatic."

"*Doddering old crone.*"

"Crone! At least I've not gone and died on some people," Nyantha sniffed.

It was all I could do not to laugh. "Okay," I said. "Where is Nyantha's frost crystal, whatever that is?"

"*It's not hers.*" Dyandrea folded her arms smugly. "*Gram gave it to me.*"

"Gram was blind as the day! You know she'd meant it for me." Nyantha huffed a breath. "The dead speak their own truth, even if they've clearly remembered it wrong," she said with a narrow-eyed glance at her sister. "You'll have to—"

"Rephrase the question. Yeah, I'd figured that much out on my own." I couldn't help a slight smile. This time I'd interrupted her, for a change. "Where is the frost crystal Nyantha wants to find?" I said.

Dyandrea scowled, and the invisible string between us jerked tighter as she strained to resist. Damn it, that still hurt—but at least it wasn't as bad as before. She eventually gave up with a drawn-out sigh. "*Stair seventy-two, buried in the wood. I've sealed it with a rune of cloaking.*"

"Finally," Nyantha breathed, and sent an over-the-top sweet smile at her sister. "Thank you, Dyandrea."

"*My pleasure,*" Dyandrea said sourly. "*Am I permitted to leave now?*"

"Well, I suppose that's up to the DeathSpeaker, if he wishes to release you." She looked at me expectantly.

"Um. Sure," I said. "Any idea how I do that?"

"*Some DeathSpeaker you are.*" Dyandrea half-smiled. "*But you've a good soul, even if you did force me to help the crone. It seems you'll do.*"

I wasn't sure I should take that as a compliment.

Nyantha shook her head. "Pay no attention to her. She means well, in her own belligerent way," she said. "I'd suggest you draw her back to you, and release her in the same manner you've done before."

"All right. I'll try."

I could still feel the unseen string, so I focused on that and imagined retracting it. The image of Dyandrea started to blur.

"Goodbye, witch," Nyantha whispered fondly.

"*Goodbye, crone.*" The words were slightly broken as the shape of her faded, leaving the cairn in its place. And the pressure in my head increased sharply. I gasped and broke the connection.

There was only a slight ache, instead of the blinding throb that usually hung around a while after I talked to the dead. No bleeding, no popped eardrums, no fishhooks in my brain. And I felt like I could've kept going with the questions, even if she'd resisted every answer.

This was so much better.

"Thank you," I said. "I can't tell you how much this means to me."

"And you'll not have to. I am psychic, after all." Nyantha extended a hand. "Now, you've some people to save, do you not?"

"Yeah. I do."

I only wished I knew how my new and improved abilities were going to help me take down the Unseelie Guard, and apparently the Queen—because last I knew, they were all still alive.

CHAPTER 22

The walk through the forest felt shorter when the banshees brought me back to Sadie and Uriskel.

They'd been waiting when Nyantha whooshed us back to the treehouse of the guardian. I'd almost wanted to stay longer—just because I still had no idea how we were going to get everyone back. But Nyantha insisted that if I trusted my abilities, everything would work out.

The DeathSpeaker does not merely speak to the dead, she'd told me. *He compels them. The dead must answer to you, and no one else. Remember that, Gideon.*

Last I'd seen her, she was climbing the steps to the treehouse, counting under her breath. That frost crystal must've been really important.

Back at the tree-cave, I was surprised to find Sadie asleep on the ground by the fire, using her backpack as a pillow. But she'd needed the rest. I suspected she was still working through the shock, and the endless hours of trudging through the swamps hadn't helped.

I wasn't surprised that Uriskel sat stiffly at the base of the tree, looking beyond annoyed as he tried to ignore the attentions of the two banshees who'd stayed behind.

Pan floated ahead into the clearing, hands on her hips. "Sisters," she said sternly. "How fare ye?"

They looked up with guilty smiles and drifted over to her, giggling.

"Good. You're back." Uriskel stood and rubbed the back of his neck, glowering at the banshees. "Wake the girl," he said. "We've a two-day hike through the marshlands before we even reach the Unseelie Wood."

"The girl is awake, thanks." Sadie opened her eyes and sat up slowly. "Did you say two days?"

"Aye. And another day to the palace, at least."

She looked like she might cry. But she pressed her lips together, pushed up from the ground and gathered her pack.

I wasn't feeling very encouraged, either.

Pan hovered on the opposite side of the fire, with the other four banshees grouped closely behind her. "Well, we've kept our word and brought ye back," she said. "If ye should find yourselves among the Trees of Ankou again, try havin' a bit of patience instead of shouting down the woods. Ye've but to call, and we'll find ye."

"Wait," I said. There had to be another way to get around this place that didn't involve a two-day slog—and maybe the banshees could help. "Can you do that thing Nyantha does? The deciding to be somewhere else thing?"

Pan shrugged. "Since I've no idea what you mean, it's likely I can't."

"Look, we've got a long way to go, and a hard fight ahead," I said. "And Uriskel doesn't even have any shoes."

"Whatever you're on about, leave me out of it," he snapped.

"What I'm saying is." I shot him a quick glare. "Is there any way you can help us get there faster?"

"Blasted—" Pan cut herself off forcefully, and ground out, "Aye. There is."

"Um...everything okay, there?" I said.

She glowered at me. "I've told ye the truth. Doesn't mean I have to like it."

Oh, right. I'd managed to forget she was dead. "Sorry," I said. "I wasn't trying to...you know. Compel you."

"Well, ye can't help that, can ye?" She relented with a wry smile. "Won't be easy, but we can take ye on the winds. Only as far as the southern border of the Unseelie Wood, though. *She* controls the skies from there."

At least I didn't have to ask who she was this time.

Uriskel gaped at me. "You're commanding banshees now?" he said. "What did you learn from this Nyantha?"

"I'll have ye know, I'm doing this as a favor," Pan huffed.

"Oh, indeed. Certainly it's nothing to do with him being the DeathSpeaker, since you're so keen on helping." He gave a faint smile. "I'll gather my things."

It didn't take long to pack. Uriskel extinguished the smoldering remains of the fire pit with a few complicated hand gestures, and Sadie gave his boots back and put her dried canvas shoes on. And we were ready.

The banshees drifted toward us, robes fluttering in an unseen breeze. "Ye'll need to hold hands," Pan said. "The journey will be...a bit rough."

"Fantastic," Uriskel grumbled. "I believe I'd rather hike the marshlands."

Sadie nudged him and took his hand. "Come on, it's not that bad," she said. "I promise we don't have cooties or anything."

He frowned. "What are cooties?"

"Seriously?"

I laughed and grabbed her other hand, then held my free hand toward him. "We're together in this," I said. "Right?"

He stared at my hand for a minute, and then took it with a firm grip. "Aye. Together."

"All sorted then, are we?" Pan said with a smile. "Hold tight, now."

Sadie squeezed my hand. "Don't let go," she whispered.

"Never."

The banshees formed a circle around us, and they joined hands, too. "Ready, sisters?" Pan said.

None of the others spoke, but I felt their assent. Especially Alice. She was practically exploding with excitement.

They started to revolve. Slowly at first, but gaining speed rapidly, until we were enclosed in a solid blur of motion. The air stirred and rustled around us. And after a minute, our feet lifted a few inches from the ground.

We hung there suspended as the banshees circled faster and the wind picked up strength, until I had to squint my eyes against it. There was a tremendous whistling sound, an almost human wailing.

Suddenly, there was nothing but the wind.

We spun and tumbled through a vortex of blinding sound, a dark strobe formed by stuttering shrieks of air. I had time to think this was probably what it felt like to get sucked into a tornado—and wonder if they had a way to land us without breaking every bone in our bodies.

Then we were standing on firm ground again, as a dying wind shivered around us.

The banshees broke apart and formed ranks behind Pan. "You lot still in one piece, are ye?" she breathed.

The three of us let go all at once, and I patted myself down with hands that trembled slightly. "Seems like it," I said. "What about you guys?"

"Fine," Uriskel said roughly.

Sadie shivered and crossed her arms. "Wow."

"That's a yes." I turned to Pan and smiled. "Thank you."

"Don't mention it. DeathSpeaker." She winked and spread her arms out. "We'll take our leave, then," she said. "Fare thee well, all of ye."

The banshees faded from sight one by one, until only Alice was left, grinning like the Cheshire cat. She giggled and waved her fingers, then pinched her nose and sank into the ground.

Leaving us to face the Unseelie Wood.

CHAPTER 23

At least the ground was dry.

Unlike the rest of Arcadia so far, the Unseelie Wood was straight out of a fairy tale—one written by the Grimm Brothers. Dark and spooky didn't even begin to describe it. The trees weren't as massive as the Trees of Ankou, but they were tall and leafless, forming random, ominous corridors. Moonlight filtered through the jagged branches to create shifting patterns along the forest floor. Quite a few of the trees wore dark green coats of moss. Rocks and boulders were common, and I spotted more than one deep cave guarded by glittering stone spires.

And there were sounds in the dark. Rustling, clicks and shuffles, the occasional distant cry of something at once mournful and chilling.

"Don't you have leaves in your realm?" I said as we passed a thick tangle of thorny, bare bushes.

Uriskel snorted. "This *is* the land of the Winter Court. Have you leaves in winter?"

"Uh, no. Guess I should be glad it's not snowing."

"Indeed, you should be." He looked around uneasily as a flurry of dry snaps echoed from somewhere. His stare settled on Sadie, and he shook his head. "That clothing," he said. "You're practically a beacon for the wild ones. Perhaps you should roll in the dirt for a bit, so at least they'd not spot you from a league away."

She frowned at him. "Are you serious?"

"Deadly."

"Wait a minute." I couldn't believe I didn't think of this before. "I can just cast a glamour on her."

Uriskel looked dubious. "Really. You are aware that laying glamour on another is quite different from generating your own," he said. "It is difficult, and the results are often muddled."

"I guess. But I've done it before."

"Have you?"

"Yeah, and I think that's a much better idea than rolling in the dirt," Sadie said as she slowed to a halt. "Go for it."

Uriskel stopped and hung back with a watchful expression.

"All right." I faced Sadie, feeling a little self-conscious with everyone staring at me. I'd go with the clothes she wore here, the ones that got destroyed when she went wolf. Black shirt and pants, green tunic, brown boots.

The moment I pictured the outfit, she was wearing it.

"Whoa." I drew back and glanced at Uriskel, who looked just as surprised. "I've never done it that way," I said. "I mean, that was fast. Usually I have to think about it a while, and concentrate, and...Jesus Christ."

Sadie stared down at herself. "Holy shit. Even Taeral can't do me like that."

Okay. I was *not* going to think about how much innuendo that statement was loaded with. "Any idea what the hell's going on?" I said to Uriskel. "It happened before, while we were hunting. That arm shield...I shouldn't have remembered the right words until I was already dead. I never do."

"It is Arcadia," he said softly. "The magic, the moonlight. You've accelerated what should have been a natural process— one you'd been denied as a changeling."

"What process?"

"The process of becoming Fae. Of using your abilities, strengthening your spark," he said. "Being here has given you all that you'd have developed, if you'd known of your heritage from the beginning."

"Hold on," I said. "You're telling me I just picked up twenty-six years of missing magic in one day?"

"Aye. And you should also have a greater understanding of the Fae language. *Bèhful grah a'gat ahn caélyn?*"

"*Tae's li moh daartheír.*" The words left my mouth angrily, before I could even think about what he'd said—or how I'd respond.

Do you love the girl?

And I'd answered *she's with my brother.*

"That much, I knew," Uriskel said with a smirk. "But you've answered my question as well."

Sadie gave me an incredulous smile. "Holy crap, Gideon. You can speak Fae already?" she said. "What did he say? What did *you* say?"

"I merely asked him how he was feeling," Uriskel said.

"Yeah." I glared at him. "And I said none of your business."

"Well, you definitely sound like a Fae." She took my hand, and I tried not to shudder too hard. "You know, maybe we can do this," she said. "The wolf is really strong over here, and you've got all this new power. And Uriskel has, um..."

"Two hundred years of hatred and rage," he intoned. "And a deck of playing cards."

"Right. That." She flashed him a look of confused sympathy, and then turned to me. "We can get them back. Can't we?"

I wanted to say yes, and mean it. But the simple little syllable refused to pass my lips. Maybe I did have more power, but I sure as hell didn't know how to use it. Except for compelling dead people. And I wasn't even sure about that. "We will," I finally said.

My hesitation had cost her some of the hope in her eyes, and I hated myself for it. I had to look away, so I lifted my gaze to the trees, trying to pull it together.

And found a pair of bright orange eyes staring down at me.

"What the hell's that?" I said, stumbling back a few steps as another set of eyes appeared just above the first. Then a third beside that one.

An awful, dry rattling sound filled the air, like a plague of demon locusts. Suddenly there were orange eyes glittering from every treetop.

I expected Uriskel to brush it off, to say they were Arcadian flying monkeys or something, just another charming fairyland critter that could probably kill us, so don't worry. And here I thought he'd said we were safe from the trees.

But he didn't brush it off. He looked downright horrified. "The Orendl," he said hoarsely. "They gather when they sense that blood is about to be shed."

Great. So they were Arcadian vultures.

"Aye, they do," a strange voice said. "But the truly unwelcome news is, ye'll be the ones to do the shedding, dearies."

All three of us turned in unison toward the sound, and I recognized the short, green-clad figure with the red hat standing in the path ahead. It was a Redcap—and not just any bad-tempered vampire leprechaun. The same one I'd bashed back across the Veil in Central Park.

And he'd brought company.

CHAPTER 24

The grinning trio behind the Redcap were Fae. I could actually sense that now—but I didn't need to, because they weren't wearing any glamour.

Two had different shades of green skin, and the third was necrotic purple. Scarified tattoos marked most of their exposed skin, including their faces. They all had pointed ears, hair like shredded vines, long arms, fingers tipped with thorns. They wore belted layers of dirty cloth and no shoes, and their eyes held a feral gleam.

So now I knew what the wild ones looked like. And for all our glamour and disguises, we didn't exactly blend.

Before anyone could react, Uriskel stepped in front of us. He was glowing, the way Taeral did when he got lethally pissed off—but his light was a dull, angry red. "I've laid claim to these outsiders," he snarled. "Touch them, and I'll scatter your entrails to the winds."

Whatever he was doing, I had a feeling they weren't in the mood to listen. I figured now was a good time to arm ourselves. I yanked my pack off, pulled it open and handed one of the guns to Sadie.

I took the dagger. At least I had a chance of hurting something with it.

The Redcap opened his too-wide mouth and laughed, showing all of his sharp, yellowed teeth. "Me wild friends are not here to challenge ye, Sidhe. We'll be takin' that one," he said, pointing a gnarled finger at me. "Ye'll not escape again, me little bargaining chip. Not when I know how truly valuable ye are to her Majesty."

Uriskel cut a glare at me. "What is this putrid halfwit babbling about?"

"I don't know, man," I said. "We ran into him in New York, months ago. He tried to take me to the Unseelie Queen then, too." I stepped forward, holding the dagger. "I think I'll pass on that, Lucky."

"What business have you with Moirehna?" Uriskel snapped at the Redcap.

"None that's yours," he said. "But as I'm a reasonable putrid halfwit, I'll make a bargain with ye." A grin crawled across his face. "Give us that, and we'll let ye and the female live—after me friends have a wee bit of fun, that is."

My gut clenched. "Over my dead body."

"Oh, we can't be havin' that. She'll want ye alive, yet." His grin vanished. "Kill the female and the Sidhe. And make that one bleed."

Damn. I really didn't want to do this.

Uriskel moved first, gesturing with both arms as he shouted, "*Céa biahn!*" All four of them flew back a good ten feet and crashed to the ground.

But they didn't stay down long.

As Uriskel charged them, Sadie took aim with the gun. In a flash it occurred to me that a gun going off in this world would draw attention we didn't want—and I had an idea of what to do about it.

I shoved the dagger in my belt and grabbed the muzzle of the gun. "*Cíunaas.*"

Sadie gave me a frantic glance. "What the hell—"

"Just shoot. And don't go wolf." I couldn't let her risk hurting someone she didn't want to. Plus, I really didn't want to get mauled.

"Fine," she spat as she pulled the trigger.

There was no sound. But one of the Fae went down with the shot.

I grinned and thrust my pack at her. "There's more ammo. Keep going," I said, and sprinted for the fight.

The other two wild Fae held Uriskel, and the Redcap was going for a bite. Remembering Sadie had said to aim for his cap the last time, I grabbed the little bastard by the arm and tore his hat off before he noticed me. It came away hard, smearing blood all over my hand.

But the bald head beneath was undamaged. It wasn't his blood.

With a hellish shriek, the Redcap wrenched from my grip and lunged at me. I sidestepped, held the bloodsoaked cap over my head—and caught sight of the Fae who'd been shot charging me from the other direction.

I gestured at him. "*Céa biahn.*"

The voice that came out of me was hollow and deep. I recognized the booming tone with a nasty start. The one I'd used the first time I accidentally called on magic against the Valentine brothers...and again when I'd removed my humanity with a drug and went full, cold-blooded Fae.

This time I didn't have a drug to blame.

The charging Fae flew through the air and smashed hard against a tree. At the same time, intense pain surged through my leg.

I glanced down to find the Redcap gnawing on my shin like a chicken bone.

"Destroy it!" Uriskel called as he elbowed one of the wild ones in the face. There was a crunch that could've been the Fae's nose breaking—or my leg. "The cap! Destroy it...it's the only way to stop him."

I could do that.

I clenched the bloody fabric tight, and the word I wanted rose instantly to my tongue. "*Saaruhtán.*"

The cap burst into flames.

I jerked my leg back with a snarl of pain, and the Redcap fell writhing to the ground. With faint horror, I watched his skin shrivel and draw tight, until it was stretched across the outline of his bones. His vast mouth opened in a silent scream as his eyes sizzled in their sockets and left blackened holes.

Nowhere near what I expected to happen.

"Gideon!"

At Uriskel's shout, I spun and ran for him at a shambling lurch, my mangled leg threatening to buckle every time it touched ground. The two he'd been fighting had him flat on the ground. I grabbed one and pulled him off, and Uriskel immediately flipped the second one and pinned him. "Kill the bastard," he snarled.

A deep part of me ached to do just that. And it terrified me.

The wild Fae ran off a few feet and turned to face me with a cold grin. I pulled the dagger, knowing he'd rush me—and he did. But my lunge missed.

His didn't. Thorny nails raked my chest, tearing the tunic and drawing blood.

I slashed at him and caught his arm. With an angry howl, he barreled into me and knocked me to the ground. Strong fingers grabbed my wrist, twisted sharply. The knife fell from my hand.

Damn it, that was *my* disarming trick.

And before I could buck him off, he rammed a knee into my groin.

Agony exploded white behind my eyes. It was slow to fade, and for a few seconds I failed to understand why I couldn't breathe—until I felt pressure on my throat, and realized he was choking me.

Coughing and struggling, I held an arm out in the direction I'd dropped the dagger and rasped the word the Unseelie soldier at the Castle had used to get his weapon back. "*Tuariis'caen.*"

The hilt slapped against my palm. I gripped it hard and drove the blade into the wild one's chest.

His grip loosened, and I rolled him over and straddled him. Pure rage flooded my veins. He'd been ready to kill my friends and deliver me to the Unseelie Queen.

I needed him dead. It was the only way to stop him.

And I knew how to do it.

With both hands wrapped around the dagger, I plunged the blade deeper and wrenched upward, through muscle and bone. The wild Fae screamed as blood poured from his mouth. Another hard thrust, and blue-white light crackled from his chest like lightning.

I'd cut the spark from his heart.

I barely realized that the wrenching cry as I yanked the blade free came from my own lips. The wild one shuddered once, and stilled forever.

Breathing harshly, I bowed my head over him and spoke the words I'd heard once from Reun—a prayer for the dead. "*Is féider leis an éirí an bóthar leat.*"

May the road rise to meet you.

"Stop him! They cannot report back to the Unseelie Court!"

Uriskel's voice seemed distant and weak. I forced myself to look, and saw one of the wild ones running away fast, despite being riddled with bullets.

I lurched to my feet and staggered toward him, holding a blood-streaked arm out, not sure what I meant to do until I spoke the spell. "*Mahrú à dionadth!*"

The shield crushed him against a nearby boulder, leaving him broken and bloodied. But not dead. He twitched feebly beneath the shimmering air, struggling in vain to free himself.

Something in me withered.

A hand clapped my shoulder. "Well done, DeathSpeaker." Uriskel, gasping for breath. "Now, finish him off."

I shivered and managed to look at him. "I can't."

His lip curled in a snarl. But as he stared at me, his features softened and he nodded once. "I'll do it, then," he said almost kindly. "Go and see to the girl."

137

I wanted to thank him. But all I could do was turn away, so I wouldn't have to watch.

CHAPTER 25

Sadie was mostly unhurt. The Fae she'd shot only came after her once, and she'd split a knuckle punching him in the jaw. Then she shot him a lot more, and he apparently decided he didn't like bullets—which was when he'd come after me.

And eventually I'd done something much worse to him.

"Let me heal that," I said, taking her hand carefully.

She gave a weak laugh. "Maybe you'd better save it for yourself. You look like hell."

"I'll be fine."

The corners of her mouth twitched. "You know, you really sound like—"

"A Fae?" I snapped.

She shivered a sigh and looked at the ground.

I hadn't meant to sound so angry. But if I tried to talk about it right now, I'd only make it worse. So I focused on healing her knuckle instead. Taeral had already taught me how to heal, and it was even easier now that the magic responded so quickly.

Still, I could feel my spark ebbing. I'd drained a lot of it during the fight, and even with the intense Arcadian moon, it would take time to recharge.

"Thank you," Sadie murmured when I lowered her hand.

I heaved a breath and looked at her. "I'm sorry," I said. "I just...really didn't want to do that. After what happened on the mountain..."

139

"And what might that be?"

Uriskel had come up beside us. His cheek was split open and bleeding freely, his shirt half torn off, and the skin of his exposed arm and part of his chest had been shredded liberally—by the wild ones' claws, I assumed. If I looked like hell, he was right there with me.

I didn't want to ask, but I had to. "Is he…"

"Aye." He grimaced and spat out a mouthful of blood. "Now, you were saying something about a mountain?"

"No. I wasn't." I turned away and limped toward the nearest tree. If I didn't sit down soon, my leg was going to drop me where I stood. I figured with the mood I was in, they'd probably leave me alone—we'd rest so Uriskel and I could heal up some, and then get moving again.

Apparently I'd figured wrong, because Uriskel followed me.

I leaned against the tree and slid gingerly to the ground. "I don't want to talk about it," I said without looking at him.

He crouched in front of me. "Well, then. I'll talk about it for you."

"What, are you psychic now?"

"This mountain," he went on like I hadn't said anything. "You killed many there, but the taste of blood was not to your liking. And so you vowed you'd not kill again."

My jaw clenched. "Sadie told you. Right?"

"No, she did not. I know this because I've been to the place I saw in your eyes, just now. That place of shame and self-loathing no amount of platitudes can ease."

I shuddered and closed my eyes. "You have no idea what I did."

"Don't I?" he said.

"I *slaughtered* people!" Now I did look at him as the rage bubbled to the surface. "I didn't just kill them. I murdered them, messy and bloody, sometimes more than one at a time. They weren't even Other. Just humans. And do you know why?" I spat. "Because they were insects. Insects with guns and clubs and Tasers and mandrake oil, and I crushed them. Because I *could*."

Uriskel raised an eyebrow. "Are you finished?"

"Yeah. Are you?"

"No." He looked hard at me. "I could tell you tales that would make your blood run cold. If you knew all that I've done, you'd find yourself a saint by comparison. But I'll not do that— and it is not because I'm in the least concerned what you think of me."

I had to admit, he probably wasn't. He'd practically gloated about what a horrible bastard he was when Taeral called him on it. "All right," I said. "Why, then?"

"Because what you feel is right," he said. "You *should* feel it. Without that remorse, you're no better than the monsters you fight. Those who seek to destroy you and the ones close to you—they feel nothing."

"So I'm better than them," I muttered. "Good for me."

"Aye. You are." He waited until I looked at him. "The warrior carves his guilt upon his heart, and he bears those scars proudly. For it is pain that drives him to action, and remorse that allows him to take lives when he's called to do so. It is his curse, but also his blessing."

"Or hers."

This time I didn't jump when Sadie spoke nearby. Uriskel tilted his head to look at her, and smiled. "Indeed. Hers as well," he said.

"Guess I'm outnumbered," I said with a smirk. "Okay, I'll try to remember that. And...thank you, Uriskel."

He nodded and rose unsteadily. "Now, we've much more to do," he said. "If you—"

"Hold on." I pushed myself up and tested my leg. At least it didn't try to fold instantly beneath me, so that was an improvement. But Uriskel didn't look even a little better. "Why aren't you healing?" I said. "Is your spark drained or something?"

141

He frowned. "I'll survive."

"You're barely standing. Maybe we should get you into moonlight, and—"

"My spark is sufficient, thank you," he said brusquely, and then looked away. "I've no healing capabilities."

"You don't?" I said. "I thought all the Fae did. Why not?"

"Because I can fly." He rolled his eyes. "Generally, all Fae have one or the other. Healing is far more common—but believe me, I am not pleased to be unique in this regard."

Sadie gaped at him. "Holy shit, you can *fly?*"

"I can," he said. "Not much use to me when I'm bleeding all over Creation, though. A state I find myself in frequently, which flight does not alleviate."

"Well then, I'll heal you."

I started for him, but he held a hand out. "I sense that your spark is low," he said. "You'll need to conserve it, in case we meet up with more wild ones."

I shook my head. "You're just as stubborn as my brother. But I've got this." I gestured at Sadie. "I can use the moonstone. Don't worry, you won't have to take it off."

"Oh, yeah," she said with a smile. "It enhances your spark, right?"

Uriskel flashed an exasperated look. "Fine. But only because you should discharge the stone's energy, so it will continue to absorb moonlight."

"Got it. Definitely not because you need help," I said, with just a touch of sarcasm. "So I'll heal you, and then we keep going. I'm up to around a fast limp right now."

"Actually, we cannot continue yet."

"Now what?"

He gestured at the scattered bodies. "The Redcap knew something of Moirehna's plans, or he'd not have sought you," he said. "We must learn what he knows. DeathSpeaker."

Oh. That.

CHAPTER 26

I was a little concerned about trying this. Nyantha's sister might have been stubborn and annoyed with me, but she wasn't evil, and she really hadn't fought too hard. I had a feeling this guy would—and I had no idea what would happen if he got away.

I'd healed Uriskel and managed to upgrade my leg from savaged to sliced, and now we stood over the desiccated corpse of the Redcap. "What happened to him, anyway?" I said. "I mean, all I did was burn his hat, and he went instant mummy."

"Redcaps thrive on the blood of their enemies," Uriskel said. "They soak their caps in it with every kill, and their own blood dries as the cap dries. If the cap is destroyed…"

"All their blood goes with it," Sadie murmured. "I'd heard about it, but I've never seen it. Jesus, look at his *eyes.*"

"Yeah." I tried not to remember watching that happen. I'd be happy going the rest of my life without seeing someone's eyes boil out of their head again. "Okay, so let's do this," I said. "Um…you might want to stand back."

I took a few steps back myself. Sadie shot me a puzzled look, and Uriskel said, "What exactly does speaking to the dead involve?"

"Well, it used to involve voices in my head, and a lot of pain and nosebleeds. But Nyantha taught me a few tricks."

Sadie knew what it was always like for me. She'd seen me drive myself to the point of blacking out—and she'd been the one trying to stop me before I got there. "So you can do it without hurting yourself now?" she said.

"Kind of."

"What do you mean, kind of?"

"You'll see." *I hope.*

I could've cheated. The body was right in front of me, and it would've been easier to just touch it and go from there. But I figured Nyantha was right. I'd never learn if I didn't practice.

Besides, I really didn't want to touch that shriveled, bloodless corpse.

Since it helped the last time, I closed my eyes. The surge of energy happened almost immediately—some part of me reaching out, rushing through the cool air. And then the sensation of my fingers brushing against a dry, leathery surface. Just as awful as I'd expected physically touching him would feel.

Which was saying a lot, considering all the corpses I'd handled over the years.

The invisible rubber band snapped back into me. And the pain was so intense, it almost drove me to my knees.

I gasped and opened my eyes as the angry soul bashed around in my mind, screaming with wordless rage that felt like ice picks through my brain. Should've planned this out a little better. I had to get him out of my head, fast. And the closest thing to project him onto was his own dead body.

"Shut up," I murmured, shaking with the effort to focus. "You want out? Here you go."

This time it happened a lot faster, and not the way I expected. The corpse plumped out and twitched once—and the dead Redcap shot to his feet. Stiff and semi-transparent, with glowing red eyes instead of holes in his skull. I could feel the unseen string that still connected me to him.

Apparently, it was a lot easier projecting a soul onto its own body.

"Oh my God!" Sadie said breathlessly as she whipped the gun back out and aimed at the apparition. "How—"

"Don't. He's still dead," I rasped. The pain was slower to fade this time, but it was already bearable. "It's just a glamour."

She lowered her arm. "You glamoured a *corpse?*"

"By the gods," Uriskel whispered. "In all my years, I've not seen such power."

"Yeah, well it's not—"

The Redcap snarled and lunged at me, driving a spike of pain through my forehead.

"Ah, *Christ*, that hurt!" I glared at the ghostly son of a bitch. "*Seabh'fóhs.*"

He stopped moving.

"You can spell the dead?" Uriskel practically stammered.

"I guess. First time I ever tried it." But I'd worry about that later. Right now, I wanted to find out what he knew and shove him back to the land of the dead—before something went wrong that I couldn't fix. "Hey. Lucky. Got some questions for you."

"*How have ye done this, boy?*" Pure fury rang through the hollow voice. "*Ye're naught but a halfling!*"

Sadie shivered beside me. "Jesus, I can hear him. Gideon..."

"Later." I didn't even want to try explaining this yet. Even though he wasn't moving, there was constant pressure on the connection, and if he got away I'd have to drag him out all over again. I decided to skip the name test. "Why were you trying to bring me to the Unseelie Queen?"

The pressure increased. "*I'd fallen out of favor with the Court,*" the Redcap said, biting back every word. "*She wanted anyone who'd come for the whore's body, and ye'd have restored me to her grace. Especially now she knows who ye are.*"

"That *whore* was my mother, you bastard," I said in a low voice. "Call her that again, and I promise your dead ass will regret it."

"*So ye are Lord Daoin's child.*" The Redcap grinned. "*Oh, but she's such plans for ye.*"

"Yeah?" I smiled back coldly. "What are they?"

"*Bastard!*" he panted as the tugging strain surged again. "*She means for Daoin...to watch ye die. As she failed to do with the...human.*"

"She tried to kill my mother?"

"*Aye, but Daoin refused to give up the wh—the one he'd taken up with. She could not break him, and so she banished him.*" The apparition frowned, and then his red eyes flared. "*DeathSpeaker,*" he said in a voice like breaking glass. "*Ye cannot be.*"

"Well, look who's caught on. Took you long enough," I said.

I felt his fear as he tried again to break free.

"Calm down, Lucky. Soon as you answer my questions, I'll let you get back to being dead." The effort of holding him was making me sweat a little, but at least it didn't hurt so much. "Why did the Unseelie Queen want to kill my mother?"

He stopped struggling. "*She wanted Daoin for herself, and he refused her.*"

Christ. I guessed royalty took rejection pretty hard. But I had to stop interrogating him about the past, and find out what he knew about the present. "Okay, listen," I said. "I can keep asking you questions and making you answer them all day, but I'd rather not. I'm sure you don't want to hang around here, either. So you tell me everything you know about what the Unseelie Queen is doing right now, and I'll release you."

The Redcap managed to look suspicious and scared. "*What she'll do to me for talking,*" he moaned. "*Pain ye cannot imagine. She can stretch it out for centuries—*"

"I guess it's a good thing you're already dead, then," I cut in. "She can't touch you now. But *I* can. So talk."

His image shivered. "*She does much. What do ye want to know?*"

"Daoin. Taeral. Reun. Anything about them."

The Redcap bowed his head. *"The Seelie noble, she's stripped him of magic and set him to…entertain the Court. As a* colhí daorii, *a—"*

"Yeah, don't finish that." A hard shudder wracked me as I understood the words. *Sex slave.* Uriskel's grimace said he caught it too, and Sadie looked horrified enough without knowing what it meant. "And Reun…agreed to this?"

"Aye, he did. She'd not relinquish Daoin, but she claimed she'd set the young lord free in exchange for the Seelie's…service. Of course, she lied. He remains in the dungeon with the cáesdhe."

Torturers.

I couldn't even look at Sadie. I knew she'd heard enough with *dungeon.* "And Daoin?" I managed through the hot lump in my throat.

"She's brought him to her chambers. None have seen him since."

"All right," I grated. "Is that all you know?"

"Wait." Uriskel took a menacing step forward. "Ask him how she knows of your presence here. *What* she knows of you."

"Since he'll only force me to, I'll answer ye," the Redcap said. *"She'd not known Daoin had two sons, until the Guard brought him in screaming that she'd never have them. That ye're in the Unseelie lands, she's only guessed, and she's put out a call to her loyal subjects to find ye. The child of Daoin— not the DeathSpeaker."* His transparent features grew solemn. *"Yet even now, the* cáesdhe *attempt to learn what the young lord knows of ye."*

I had to close my eyes briefly. "Anything else I should know?"

"Aye. Ye should leave them for dead and return to the human realm, dearie," he said. *"For if she takes ye, death will seem a great comfort by comparison."*

"Yeah, that's not happening," I said. "Goodbye, Lucky."

I yanked him back, ignoring the pain as his soul crowded into my head. The apparition folded to the ground and reverted to a lifeless corpse, and I released him to whatever the world of the dead had in store.

Here in the land of the living, I had some friends to save.

CHAPTER 27

Under different circumstances, the small, crackling fire might've been cheerful.

We'd been walking through the woods for hours, not talking much after the Redcap's gruesome confessions. At least there hadn't been any more attacks or creepy orange eyes staring down from the trees. Uriskel had finally called a halt, allegedly for the night—though it wasn't any different than the day. Same moon, same unsettling dark light. While I was visiting Nyantha, he'd prepared and packed meat from the animal we'd hunted, so we warmed some up and ate what we could.

No one had much of an appetite, though. Not even Sadie.

I stretched and wiped my greasy hands on my pants. Didn't really matter, since all of us were covered with varying degrees of grime and blood—though Sadie's wasn't visible on the glamour clothes. I'd recast the spell a few hours ago when it started to fade. "So," I said. "Aren't we giving away our position with the fire, or something?"

Uriskel started, like he was coming back from somewhere far away. "More likely we'd be noticed without one," he said. "Fires are common here. We've a lack of central heating in Arcadia."

"Right. I guess I've watched too many movies." More than usual lately, thanks to Daoin's obsession. That hurt to think about. The idea that the Unseelie Queen was doing God knew what to him, the way he was now…childlike, easily confused, and probably terrified. He wouldn't understand why any of it was happening. And what she'd done to Taeral and Reun was just as unspeakable.

Sadie stirred and looked across the fire. "Can I ask you something, Uriskel?"

"I suppose."

I glanced at her uneasily. She hadn't said a word about Taeral since the Redcap, and I was worried she'd ask his opinion on our chances. They probably weren't too high—and he wouldn't hesitate to share them. But she frowned slightly, and said, "I've been thinking about something you said that doesn't make sense. Something about having two hundred years of hatred, and a deck of cards?"

He sighed. "I did say that, didn't I. How foolish of me."

"It's okay. You don't have to explain," she said. "It was just...weird."

"Aye, it is a strange tale." He paused, and then dragged his pack beside him and took something out of it. A weathered, battered leather case about the size of a pack of cigarettes, with black scorch marks along the edges. "I'd been thrown in gaol," he said, turning the pack over slowly in his hands. "For...something I'd done. But gaol here is not like your jails in the human realm."

"Yeah, I could've guessed that," I said. "You have dungeons."

He smirked without looking up. "The Seelie dungeons might've been preferable," he said. "A gaol is a covered hole in the ground, which you're forced to dig yourself. Prisoners are fed and given water once a day...if the guards remember, or bother. There is no light, no sound, no contact with anyone." He stared into the fire. "They left me there for five years."

Jesus. I couldn't imagine anything that sounded worse than a dungeon, until that.

"The prince, Braelan—at the time, he'd not known we were brothers. In fact he despised me. He'd been raised in the Summer Court, trained to hate and fear the Unseelie. The King encouraged him to treat me as he did. Like a vicious dog who might turn on its masters at any moment." He opened the pack slowly and drew out a deck of cards. They were ragged, faded, and very old. Smaller and thicker than modern cards, and simply designed, like something out of an Old West saloon. "Even the prince felt sorry for me, and they'd told him my sentence was only one year—twice as long as the maximum six-month sentence the Court usually hands down. And so, he gave me these to occupy my time."

"You spent five years alone in a hole?" Sadie shuddered. "I knew the Seelie were cruel, but that's just...above and beyond. Deck of cards or not."

Uriskel nodded once and replace the cards. "I did deserve it," he said hoarsely. "Perhaps not five years of it, but...at any rate, I spent all that time enchanting the cards. I'd nothing better to do. And now, each one is a spell far more powerful than I'm capable of casting with raw magic."

Somehow I doubted he'd deserved a punishment like that, but I wouldn't mention it. I knew he'd only brush me off, and whatever it was obviously still hurt him. Instead I said, "So you've got something that'll help us against the Unseelie Court in there, right?"

His smile was gentler this time. "Aye. A few things."

"Like, stripping someone's magic?" I said. "The Redcap said that's what the Queen did to Reun. If you can do that, and maybe tell me how..."

He was already shaking his head. "You'd not be able to learn," he said. "Only those with full royal blood can deny another Fae's magic."

Well, that sucked.

Then I thought about what he'd actually said. Not that he couldn't do it—only that I wouldn't be able to learn. And he said 'full royal blood.' If the Seelie King was his father, and he was half Unseelie...

I tried to piece together what he said to Cobalt, when I couldn't understand enough Fae. The angry, disgusted words that made Cobalt grudgingly change his mind about him coming here. One of the words was Moirehna. It meant nothing at the time, but now I knew who he'd been talking about. *Táe mihc Moirehna, amain oídreh riicthaiorn. Cuimmáihg, daartheír?*

I am the son of Moirehna, the sole heir to the throne. Remember, brother?

And I knew why Cobalt said that Uriskel might have a way to get us out.

"Holy hell," I said. "The Unseelie Queen is—"

"I'd greatly prefer you did not mention that," Uriskel growled. "There are few who know, and I've no wish for it to become common knowledge."

"All right," I said carefully. "Consider it not mentioned."

"Thank you. Now, I suggest you both rest while you can. We've still quite a journey ahead of us." He stood, grabbed his pack and walked a few feet away, then sat down with his back turned.

Sadie stared at me. "What the hell was that about?" she whispered.

"I guess he's got some family issues," I replied in kind.

"Yeah, join the club." She shrugged and stretched her arms over her head. "Maybe we should get some sleep," she said. "Or try to, anyway."

Unfortunately, I doubted that was going to happen.

———————◆———————

A few hours later, I was unhappy to learn that I'd been right. No way was I getting to sleep.

I sat up slowly from the ground, trying not to disturb Sadie. At least one of us was resting. Uriskel was stretched out at a distance. I couldn't tell if he was asleep, but he didn't seem to notice when I stood and walked slowly away from the fire. Or maybe he didn't care.

Good thing I knew he wasn't as heartless as he wanted everyone to think, or I would've been pissed.

We'd passed a small stream just before we made camp. I headed that way, thinking I'd get a drink and try to wash up a little. Maybe the filth helped us blend in, but I wasn't in the mood to be this...wild.

It reminded me too much of the Valentines.

Bathing only happened after a hunt, and the hunts usually lasted for days, or weeks. The dirtier everyone was, the better they could hide the scent of human from their prey. And since all the nasty jobs fell to me, I'd spend the majority of my time smeared stiff with blood, dirt, entrails, and shit of every variety.

That was probably why I'd developed a two-shower-a-day habit once I got away from them. And I was itching to get this crap off me.

The stream was maybe three feet wide and about as deep, fast-running but not whitewater rapids speed. Crystal clear water revealed a stream bed of smooth, loose rocks, and thick grass-like plants with dark blue stalks grew to a height of four or five feet along the opposite bank. But this side was clear.

I knelt beside the stream, splashed water on my face, and drank until my stomach was tight. Then I plunged my hands into the cold flow and tried to rub some of the grime away. It didn't come off easy. But I did the best I could with my exposed skin, including my face and neck.

While I was here, I figured I'd try to wash the shirts, at least. The wild Fae had torn through both of them with his claws, and they were crusted with dirt and blood—mine, and his. I wanted that off, at least. I removed the tunic and the long-sleeved shirt beneath, hesitated a minute, and plunged them both in the stream. They'd dry eventually.

Just as I finished wringing them out, a voice behind me said, "I thought your tattoos were supposed to glow."

"Damn it, Sadie!" I held my breath until my heart crawled out of my throat, and then let it out slowly. "Would you *please* learn to make some noise."

"I'm sorry." At least she sounded like she meant it this time. I heard her footsteps as she walked up beside me and crouched by the stream. "Seriously, though," she said. "They're not glowing."

I managed half a smile. "I guess that means I'm not almost dead, and you're not here to harm me."

"Right on both counts." She let out a sigh and trailed a hand in the water, staring intently at the opposite bank. "I take it you couldn't sleep?" she said.

"Not even a little."

"I think I was dozing. Not sleeping, exactly. I heard you get up." She still wouldn't look at me. I wondered what was wrong, besides the obvious, until she said, "Aren't you going to get dressed? I know you don't like people...looking at you."

"Oh." I shook out the shirt and pulled it on, shivering a little as the frigid dampness slapped against my skin. "Better?"

"Gideon." She turned slowly to face me. "It's not me with the problem," she said. "Don't you know that?"

"Yeah, I get it. It's not you. It's me."

"You're not ugly."

Hell if I wasn't. But this was not a conversation I wanted to have, so instead of challenging her, I struggled back into the damp, heavy tunic and got to my feet. "If you want a drink or something, go ahead. I'll wait," I said. "It's probably better if we walk back together."

She tilted a look at me, and then stood with a determined expression. "Gideon, you are *not* your scars."

"Damn it, I'm not doing this," I said. "You don't know shit about it, and—"

"I would if you told me."

"—and I want to keep it that way!" I couldn't stand glaring at her for long, so I dropped my gaze to the ground. "Do you think I *want* you to know my pathetic story? To believe that every time you look at me, you probably want to cry, or puke?" I managed to lift my head. "Because for a long time that's all I could think when I looked in a mirror, or took a shower, or changed my clothes. I never wanted anyone to look at me, at *this*, and have to carry the burden of *why*. That's my goddamn burden. And there is no fucking why."

"All right," she said shakily. "But just so you know, that's what friends are for. To help carry the burden."

I blew a frustrated breath. Hurting her, scaring her—that wasn't my intention. She was scared enough as it was. "Look, I just...they were hunters." I couldn't believe I was telling her anything, even as the words left my mouth. "The family I grew up with, the one I thought actually was my family," I said. "Not weekend hunters, but full-time, big-game poachers dealing in the black market. They lived in a camper caravan and moved around constantly. Across the country, up into Canada, down to Mexico a few times. Anywhere dangerous and untamed, where normal people wouldn't go. Kind of like Arcadia." I paused, trying to unclench my jaw. "And they hated my guts. Every last one of them."

She bit her lip. "Gideon, I'm sor—"

"Please. Don't be sorry. That's the last thing I want." Now I felt bad for basically saying I didn't want to be here, because it wasn't true. The landscape was never my problem. "We're going to find him, Sadie," I said. "I promise we'll get him back."

"Oh God, don't promise." With a small smile, she reached out and brushed her fingers along the side of my face. Her touch practically burned me. "It might kill you," she half-whispered. "And I couldn't stand to lose you, too."

Christ, this was not good. I couldn't come up with a thing to say—and if I didn't start talking, I was going to do something monumentally stupid. Like kiss my brother's girlfriend while he was off being tortured.

Before I could start babbling something, anything to break me from looking into her eyes and wanting her, we were interrupted by something equally bad. A rustling-grass sound from somewhere behind me, followed by a sharp splash.

Sadie stepped back with a gasp, her horrified gaze rooted to whatever made the noise. And I really didn't want to look.

"Oh my God," she choked out. "Taeral!"

REALM OF MIRRORS

CHAPTER 28

I was moving the instant his name left her lips.

It was him. Barely conscious and without his glamour, shirtless and shoeless, missing his arm, and so badly beaten that just looking at him was physically painful—but alive. Breathing.

He'd landed half in the stream with his face barely above water. I jumped in without hesitation, got behind him and wrapped both arms around his torso, wincing in sympathy at all the ways I was probably hurting him. But he didn't so much as flinch.

Sadie was in the water before I finished lifting him. Tears streaked her face, and she moaned as she went for his legs. "We're going to make him worse, just touching him," she said. "Oh, God, those *bastards.*"

"I know. But we can't let him drown."

Between us, we maneuvered him carefully to the clear side of the stream. "Should we put him down here?" Sadie whispered.

I wanted to. But we'd be safer by the fire—if there was anywhere safe in these woods. "No," I said. "We have to get him back."

She nodded reluctantly and shifted her grip, easing an arm beneath his knees to put less pressure on him. "Let's go, then."

It took a lot longer than I wanted to make the distance to camp. We had to move slowly, try not to jostle him. Taeral's body remained rigid as stone the entire time, every muscle constantly vibrating. He didn't open his eyes or make a single sound.

The instant we were in sight of the banked fire, Uriskel was on his feet and striding rapidly toward us. "What's happened?" he called. "Tell me you did not run into—" He came to an abrupt halt when he was close enough to see what we carried. "Is that Taeral?"

"Yeah," I said. "He's alive."

Without a word, Uriskel scooped him effortlessly from us, then turned and carried him back to the fire at twice the speed we'd managed.

Okay, so he was cranky, powerful, and strong as a bull too.

Sadie and I rushed to catch up as Uriskel knelt and laid him gently on the ground. Then he sent an angry glare over his shoulder. "Was he followed?"

That wasn't a question I expected. "Um, no," I said. "There wasn't anyone else."

"You're certain of this."

"He was alone! What's *wrong* with you?" Sadie narrowed her eyes and rushed to Taeral's other side, taking a knee beside him. "Did you even look at him?"

"Aye, I did," Uriskel said evenly. "So tell me...how could he have possibly escaped the dungeon in this condition? Unless they allowed him to, so they could follow him."

Everything he said was logical, and it was something we really needed to consider. But it still pissed me off. I didn't *want* to give a damn how he got here—I just wanted to be grateful that he had. "Look, it's just him," I said. "And even if he was followed, and they're waiting to jump us right now, what do you want to do about it? Leave him here and run?"

For a second, I thought I saw just that in his eyes. Then he surrendered and straightened with a heavy sigh. "Heal him, if you can," he said. "I'll be out casting wards. For all of eternity." He shook his head, turned on a heel and stalked away, muttering something under his breath about trying to ward the entire Unseelie Wood.

Considering the circumstances, I thought he'd taken it pretty well.

———————◆———————

I'd used up most of my spark and all the energy stored in the moonstone twice, but Taeral was still unconscious.

At least he looked a little less like a prop corpse from the world's most sadistic horror movie. His breathing was a bit more natural, his body relaxed, and some of the bruising and swelling had gone down. Sadie had tried to dab the blood off with one of her t-shirts and water from the canteen, but she couldn't bear to do it for long, in case he felt it.

Now she sat on the ground holding his hand. I was on his other side, and Uriskel huddled across the fire from us, slowly building the flames back up. He must've decided to only cast wards for part of eternity.

Once my spark recharged, I'd try again. For the moment, it was all I could do not to start screaming—and never stop.

I didn't think I'd ever felt this…much. It was the only way to describe the awful, writhing mass that formed inside me the instant I'd seen him, and refused to ease. I was horrified at the pain he must've gone through. Practically relieved to tears that he was still alive. So furious at the people who'd done this to him, the anger was a hot blade in my gut.

And utterly sickened that one of my first, short-lived thoughts was to take him back to the human realm, right now, while we still could. Without Daoin and Reun.

I'd dismissed the idea almost as soon as it came. But I still hated myself for having it.

"Do you think they poisoned him?"

Sadie's broken whisper distracted me from my self-loathing. "I don't know," I said slowly. "But that's a good point." If he was dosed with cold iron or mandrake oil, healing magic wouldn't cancel the effects. Only time could do that—something we probably didn't have much of.

159

I heard Uriskel rifling around in his pack for something. A minute later, he walked around the fire holding a large silver flask. "If he's poisoned, this'll help," he said as he tossed the flask to me.

"What is it?"

"Self-medication." He gave a crooked smile. "It's elderberry wine."

I almost refused. Taeral had a problem with alcohol, and I didn't think getting him drunk was the best idea right now. But then I remembered the first time I'd seen him shot with a cold iron bullet. He'd brought out a bottle and Sadie started giving him hell for drinking, until he told her it was elderberry wine—and it would neutralize the poison.

Sadie's expression said she remembered that, too.

"Thank you," I said. "I'm glad you packed this. What made you think of it?"

"Mere habit." Uriskel shrugged. "With no healing abilities, I've a need to rely on alternative methods. Sometimes the only option is to deal with the pain," he said. "Wine helps with that too, even if I've not been poisoned. And I do enjoy the taste."

And now I felt bad again. "Well, I'll try to make sure there's some left for you."

He waved a dismissive hand. "Use it all," he said. "I can always raid my brother's supply when we return."

I couldn't help noticing he'd said when, not if. Like maybe he thought we had a chance now.

With a nod of thanks, I shuffled on my knees behind Taeral's head and propped him against my thighs, so he wouldn't choke on the stuff. I uncapped the flask and opened his mouth carefully.

Not much of it went down at first. Most of the deep red liquid dribbled down his chin and from the sides of his mouth, looking uncomfortably like blood. I tilted his head back a little further and tried to drip it directly down his throat.

His body tensed. He coughed and spluttered, and his eyes flew open. But I didn't think he was seeing anything—they were glassy and unfocused, watering with pain.

"Taeral." Maybe he could hear me. "Can you drink this? It should help."

He gave a bare nod, the slightest shift of his head. I really hoped that meant yes.

This time when I tipped the flask, he managed to swallow a few times before the coughing started again. I moved it away until he stopped. "Did they poison you?"

Another weak nod.

"All right. Try to get this down."

He drank a little more, and then shuddered and blinked slowly. When he opened his eyes, they focused on Uriskel standing a few feet away.

"*You.*" His voice was a rusted scrape, like a knife against stone. "Bastard. How could you...bring him here?"

I felt the words like a blow, and they weren't even directed at me. I was too stunned to say anything.

Uriskel's expression gave away nothing, but now I knew him well enough to understand how furious he really was. He stared at Taeral for a long time, like he was trying to decide whether to scream at him, or kill him.

Finally, he said, "You're welcome."

And he walked away.

CHAPTER 29

I had to give Taeral the short version of why he shouldn't try to get up and kill Uriskel, other than the fact that he physically couldn't. He calmed down a little at the halfling part, and a lot more when I mentioned two hundred years of slavery to the Seelie Court.

Now he was mostly pissed at me.

"Why did you come here? Both of you could have been killed."

"You know why," I said.

"I sensed you in the woods, but I…did not believe it." His head fell back, and he closed his eyes with a grimace. "*A'ghreal.*"

Sadie squeezed his hand. "I'm here."

"I know." One corner of his mouth lifted slightly. "You should not be."

"You know, I'm really trying not to get angry at you," she said. "You're crazy if you think I was going to sit around—"

"But." The soft word got her attention. "I am grateful to see you both."

Well, that was a first. He'd backed down from stubborn in record time.

"Get more of that wine down him, will you?" Uriskel materialized from the other side of the fire and tossed something at me—a leaf-wrapped portion of meat. "And eat, if you can. Young lord."

Taeral shuddered and strained to sit up. "Uriskel... *ihmpáeg míe d'maihtúnaas.*"

I beg your forgiveness. Pretty sure that was a first, too.

Uriskel sighed. "No need," he said. "Fortunately for you, I've a brother of my own who's just as bullheaded as yours. I'd have said the same, or worse, if you'd been the one bringing him into danger."

"Bullheaded?" I echoed.

"Aye. You are." Taeral's smirk turned into a wince. He almost fell back again, but he managed to catch himself. "Well, I thank you anyway," he said to Uriskel. "I'd no idea—"

"Yes, let's dispense with talk of my sad little tale," Uriskel said abruptly. "You can thank me by telling me how you've escaped the palace dungeon, so I'm assured that you were not followed."

His brow furrowed. "How did you know where I was?"

"A dead guy told us," I said. "Little Redcap bastard, big mouth. He...told us about Reun, too."

Taeral's jaw clenched. "Aye, the fool. He should've known not to take Moirehna at her word, yet he still offered himself for me," he said. "Gideon...any word of our father?"

Damn, I wished I had better news. "Only that no one's seen him."

"I thought as much." Something dark flashed in his eyes. "She'll not kill him. But she will destroy him, and soon." He frowned and looked at Uriskel. "As to my escape, that was Levoran's doing. One of the Unseelie Guard, my father's lieutenant," he said. "Even now he remains loyal to our family. He'll suffer greatly when she discovers what he's done," he added in a rough whisper.

"I suppose that's acceptable." Uriskel folded his arms. "Still...how soon can you move? Even with the wards, we should not linger here."

Sadie opened her mouth angrily, but Taeral stopped her with a shake of his head. "He is right. Her spies travel these

163

woods, always." He raised his hand and flexed it slowly, and I realized with a nasty start that at least two of his fingers were broken. But he hadn't protested Sadie holding his hand. "I assume the plan is to get to the palace?" he said.

"Aye. More or less."

"Well, I'm worse than useless without my arm. They've destroyed it." He gritted his teeth, tried to stand, and gave up with a gasp. "I must replace it," he said. "We'll need every advantage if we're to survive."

"I admit, that was a splendid piece of work," Uriskel said. "Where in Arcadia did you get it?"

Taeral gave a soft, bitter laugh. "The mirror mender."

"No." Uriskel immediately backed up a step, one hand extended in protest. "Gods, no. We're not engaging with that mad old relic. Besides, the Autumn Highlands are a three-day journey from here—and that's under ideal conditions."

Okay. So the mirror mender was bad news, whoever that was.

"The Highlands are neutral ground," Taeral said. "We'll be safe there, for a time. And it need not take three days. Those with royal blood can open a direct portal to...oh." His shoulders slumped. "Those with *full* royal blood."

I cleared my throat loudly. "Neutral ground seems like a good idea to me," I said, looking hard at Uriskel. "And we do need all the help we can get."

"Blasted, meddlesome fledgling! I've no interest in—" He cut himself off with a frustrated growl. "Fine," he spat. "Neutral ground it is. But I'll not speak to that daft, chirping monstrosity. Nor will I drink any of her dreadful tea."

Taeral stared at him. "You are a full royal?"

"It would seem so," he said through his teeth. "And since we're traveling by portal, we've no need to wait. So let's get this over with."

As he strode around the fire, probably to gather his pack, I moved to help Taeral stand. "Um...what dreadful tea?" I said.

"The mirror mender is difficult to explain." He let me place his arm around my shoulders, and Sadie circled him to hover nervously on his other side. "Nearly impossible, in fact," he said. "She is…something you must experience for yourself."

I wasn't sure I liked the idea of experiencing someone. It sounded a lot worse than meeting them.

Somehow, we managed to get Taeral on his feet. He couldn't stay there without support, so Sadie grabbed our gear while I kept an arm around him, trying to avoid the worst of the damage. "Do I even want to know what they did to you?" I said quietly.

He shook his head. "Easier to tell you what they've *not* done to me. The *cáesdhe* are… quite skilled in their profession."

"All right." I tried for a light tone, but my voice shook anyway. "What didn't they do to you, then?"

"They did not break me." His expression hardened. "And I'll not allow them to break Daoin, either."

"You mean *we* won't," I said.

His smile temporarily banished the pain in his eyes. "Aye, brother. We will not."

"If you're through…bonding?" Uriskel's dry tone cut in. He stood in front of us, pack in place and the ghost of a smile on his lips. "The rest of us are ready."

"Yeah, we're done," I said. "Let's do this."

CHAPTER 30

The mirror mender lived in a castle straight out of Sleeping Beauty.

Uriskel's portal worked the same as the one that brought us to Arcadia. We stepped out into a vast, walled courtyard paved with gray stone and overgrown with bramble weeds. They snaked across the stone floor, curled and tangled around free-standing archways, and choked a scattering of statues and fountains that were slowly crumbling with neglect.

There wasn't a sound in the place.

"I don't think anyone's home," Sadie said in strained tones. "This place smells...wrong. I mean, it's like *nothing* has ever been here."

I had to agree. Definitely a creepy, don't-go-in-the-basement kind of feeling.

Uriskel gave a derisive snort. "Of course she's here," he said. "This is all part of her blasted production. Every visit is a grand event, or some such royal nonsense."

"Are you sure about that?" I said.

"Unfortunately." With a barely contained groan, Uriskel clomped across the courtyard toward the equally creepy castle.

"It is true." Taeral sounded faintly amused. "She does enjoy showing off."

"If you say so."

I couldn't imagine what kind of showing off something like this would involve. But we made our way to the ominous structure, and I thought Taeral was leaning a little less on me now. At least, I hoped he was improving.

The castle itself was alabaster stone, dulled to a menacing yellow and streaked liberally with grime. Ragged vines hung listlessly from the tops of the turrets and fringed the edges of the roof. There were three lines of runes carved above the vast, arched wooden door. I couldn't understand them as easily as the spoken language, but I managed to puzzle them out.

Mirror Mender

Royal Tailor and Chief Artificer of the Courts of Arcadia

Welcome, Noble Guests

I had no idea what an artificer was, but it sounded kind of...stuffy.

Uriskel gripped the huge iron ring mounted on the door and glanced back with a pained expression. "Are you certain we've a need to do this?" he said. "I've contacts in the Gray Market. Surely we could find something suitable there."

"Go on," Taeral said. "It's not *that* bad."

"Isn't it?" He sighed deeply, turned back to the door and banged the ring against it three times. The hollow booms echoed in the stillness of the courtyard.

The door creaked slowly open onto darkness.

"Oh, come on," Sadie said. "You're telling me that's not suspicious?"

Uriskel rolled his eyes and walked inside. After a brief hesitation, we followed.

The interior of the place was even worse than the outside. Dull, ambient light with no apparent source revealed a cavern of a main room with an enormous crystal chandelier suspended in the center of a high ceiling, and a wide marble staircase at the far end with a landing halfway up, where more stairs split off to the left and right. Thick layers of dust and massive, intricate cobwebs in fans and sheets covered everything.

And rows of motionless silhouettes stood guard at the edges of the room, just beyond the faint light.

"May I help you?"

The voice, like personified thunder speaking through a mouthful of molasses, came from a pocket of gloom to the right of the door. I focused on the spot and made out a misshapen slab of a man, almost as tall as Taeral and twice as wide. He was completely bald, with a craggy brow, deep-set eyes, and huge, square teeth that leaned like a rotted picket fence. One shoulder was higher than the other. His forearms bulged with a network of raised veins, and his feet were the size of hams.

Great. The mirror mender's butler was Igor on steroids.

"We've come for the services of the mirror mender." Uriskel spoke in a tone I'd never heard from him before. Cold and dismissive, almost haughty. "Present us at once."

Igor the Terrible looked unimpressed. "Speak the phrase, then," he said. "All those who seek audience with—"

"Yes, I am aware of the protocol." Uriskel's jaw clenched hard. "*Deínahm alaen doun.*"

Make me beautiful?

"Welcome, noble guests." Igor bowed deeply, and then pulled a tattered velvet cord I hadn't noticed hanging beside him. It rang the loudest bell I'd ever heard, with enough force to shake a shower of dust from the chandelier.

"Oh, joy," Uriskel murmured. "We've been granted an audience. How fortunate."

I would've said something back, but I was busy staring at the impossible thing sliding down the left staircase to stop on the landing. It looked like a pile of jumbled scrap metal in the dim light. When it stopped, a pair of torches flared to life behind it.

The mirror mender was a person-sized robot spider.

Okay, maybe spider was the wrong word. It—she—was made of metal. A vaguely human-shaped torso floated a few inches above something that looked like the bottom half of a mermaid, except with the tail of a snake instead of a fish. A large, round crystal ball, glowing a pale blue, nestled at the top of the gap where her waist should've been, just below the narrow point of the torso. A similar crystal rested at the top of her neck, and the head floating above it was insectile, with closed mandibles and three jeweled eyes—two in the normal places, and the other centered on her forehead.

She had two segmented metal arms in front. And eight or ten more sprouting from her back, each tipped with an...implement. Scythes, pincers, hooks, pointed rods, and at least one that looked like scissors.

Her eyes flashed four times. Once for each of us. And as she slithered soundlessly down the main staircase, she spoke in a metallic and measured voice, like an automated phone recording or a badly programmed GPS.

"PRINCE URISKEL. LORD TAERAL. AND GUESTS. WEL-COME, WEL-COME." Her wasp-like mouth didn't move with the monotone words—and the effect was chilling. "I DO HOPE YOU HAVE BROUGHT ME A CHALLENGE."

"We have." Straining with effort, Taeral pushed away and managed to stand on his own. "The arm you crafted me has been...damaged," he said. "If it pleases you, I'd like a replacement."

"WONDERFUL. WONDERFUL." Her eyes flashed again. "BUT YOU ARE IN SUCH A STATE. NONE OF YOU WILL LEAVE UNTIL I HAVE CLOTHED YOU IN A FITTING MANNER."

"That won't be necessary," Uriskel said flatly.

"I INSIST. THIS IS NO WAY FOR A PRINCE TO DRESS." Her head bobbed down in disapproval. "OH, BUT WE WERE NOT EXPECTING SUCH NOBLE COMPANY. WERE WE, SHARDE."

Apparently that was Igor's name, because he shambled closer and said, "No, mistress. 'Tis a pleasant surprise."

"FORGIVE ME. YOU MUST GIVE ME A MOMENT TO TIDY UP."

The mirror mender clapped her flat, hinged hands together.

An explosion of light rippled outward from her, filling the great room with brilliance. And when it faded, all the dust and cobwebs went with it. The chandelier blazed to life, transforming the gloomy cavern to a breathtaking showplace of a palace, dripping with luxurious reverence. Gleaming marble, polished wood and brass, silk banner draped from the ceiling and over the rails of the upper balcony. The frozen silhouettes around the edge of the room were mannequins—male and female, eerily lifelike, and wearing the kind of outfits I'd only seen in movies. All dolled up for the royal ball.

Standing there made me feel underdressed, even though I'd never cared about formalities like that in my life.

"WAKE UP. WAKE UP, EVERYONE." With strangely graceful movements, the mirror mender drifted around the borders of the room, touching a select few of the exquisite female mannequins.

Each one she touched came to attention, stepped off its pedestal, and followed the royal tailor as she added more attendants to the parade.

"Oh, fantastic," Uriskel groaned. "Nymphs."

The last mannequin she brought to life was a male, dressed in a midnight blue suit with long coattails over a white shirt with frilled lace cuffs, open at the throat. She returned to the center of the room, facing us, and the small army gathered behind her.

"PLEASE. STEP INTO MY PARLOR," the mirror mender said in her droning, machine-like voice. "WE HAVE SO MUCH TO DISCUSS. AND AS FORTUNE FAVORS US, IT HAPPENS TO BE TEA TIME."

I was too fascinated to even think about refusing.

CHAPTER 31

The parlor was just as decadent as the great room, and I felt even more like a scrub.

Four cushioned chairs, arranged in a semi-circle, were somehow waiting for us when Sharde showed us into the room. Taeral had started to flag and stumble, and Sadie helped him into the second chair before settling in the first. She hadn't said a word since the appearance of the mirror mender, and she still looked half-stunned.

I sat beside Taeral, and Uriskel reluctantly took the last seat. "I'll not escape this, will I?" he said, leaning forward slightly to look across me at Taeral. "You *know* what she'll demand as payment."

"Aye, and I hope you've something to give her," he replied. "I've not set foot in Arcadia for thirty years, now."

Uriskel huffed and folded his arms. "Splendid. I suppose I've no choice, then."

I frowned. "What are we supposed to pay her with?"

"Her most valued coin in trade," Taeral said with a sidelong smile. "Royal gossip."

Before I could think too hard about that, the mirror mender swept in with a cloud of nymphs at her heels—well, her tail. Two of them pushed a wheeled silver cart in front of us, laden with...tea things. A large ceramic pot, a collection of lidded canisters, stacks of delicate porcelain cups and saucers, a bowl of glittering sugar cubes.

Uriskel actively tried to disappear into his chair.

The mirror mender glided to the other side of the cart, emitting a strange, tuneless hum. "WHAT SHALL WE SERVE. PRIMROSE. BLUEBELL." She lifted various lids from canisters and put them back. "NO. BLACKTHORN AND WILD THYME. QUITE FITTING FOR THE OCCASION."

And she went to work.

All of her arms moved at once, almost faster than I could follow. One of them produced a steady jet of fire beneath the teapot while the rest placed cups on saucers and measured powders into cups, preparing four of them in a complicated dance of clicking, clattering metal. Her torso bobbed up and down rhythmically, and the tuneless hum evolved into a series of chirps and fluttering trills, like a whole flock of songbirds.

The instant the teapot whistled out steam, her extra arms snapped back into place. She picked up the pot with her front hands and serenely poured water into the cups, one at a time. "WONDERFUL. WONDERFUL," she said. "THE TEA IS READY."

Four pincer arms snaked from her back. With perfect synchronization, each of them dropped a lump of sugar in a cup, picked up a spoon and stirred the brew, and extended a cup and saucer to each of us—except Taeral, who only got a cup.

"Thank you," Sadie and I murmured at the same time, while Taeral offered a slow nod and a smile. Uriskel just glared a lot.

I figured it couldn't be as dreadful as Uriskel insisted it was. It was only tea, after all, and there was sugar in it. So I blew on the steaming liquid for a minute, took a tentative sip— and damn near gagged.

Okay, it was worse than dreadful. The stuff tasted like hot, sugary dirt.

The mirror mender flashed her eyes at me. "HOW IS YOUR TEA, YOUNG MASTER."

"Delightful," I managed to squeak out. I'd just stop blowing on it and drink it fast. Maybe that way it'd burn my tongue, and I wouldn't have to taste it.

Taeral's eyes held restrained amusement. Somehow he drank normally without choking, and then raised his cup in a salute. "Refreshing, as always," he said smoothly. "I do enjoy a good spot of tea."

Sadie shot a glance at him and sipped from her cup. Then she closed her eyes for a long moment. "It's sweet," she finally said with a slight cough. "And...earthy."

Everyone looked at Uriskel.

He made a low sound deep in his throat, and tossed the entire cup down like a shot. "I've a friend who would call this bloody fantastic," he rumbled, and added under his breath, "Though I'd not."

The mirror mender bobbed her head and managed to look pleased. "SPLENDID. SPLENDID. ANOTHER CUP THEN, PRINCE URISKEL."

His lip curled as he extended the cup and saucer toward her. "It would be my pleasure," he forced out.

"MARVELOUS." Her many arms whirled into motion again. "I HAVE ALREADY PLANNED THE PERFECT OUTFIT FOR EACH OF YOU. AND IF I MAY BE SO BOLD, I SHOULD LIKE TO CONFER WITH THE PRINCE AND THE LORD TO DISCUSS PAYMENT. SHARDE. PLEASE ALLOW OUR YOUNG MASTER AND MISTRESS TO EXPLORE THE GROUNDS."

The expression on Uriskel's face clearly said *kill me now*.

I hadn't even seen Sharde come back into the room. But suddenly the butler, or whatever he was, stood beside the chairs with his hands behind his back. "If you'll kindly come with me," he said. There was no request in his tone.

Sadie and I both got up, and two metal arms whisked our cups away. "THANK YOU. THANK YOU," the mirror mender said. "SHARDE WILL OF COURSE SUMMON YOU, WHEN YOUR GARMENTS ARE READY."

She was still madly preparing tea as we followed Sharde out.

"How much longer do you think they'll be?"

Sadie sat next to me on the ground beneath a leafless, silver-white tree, fidgeting nervously with the moonstone. It'd been hours since Sharde showed us through a back door into a vast, meticulously tended yard with multiple gardens and rolling stretches of grass. Whatever the mirror mender had done to transform the inside of the castle, the same thing had happened outside. Now it was all gleaming white stone and fertile landscape.

We'd already walked a full circuit of the stone wall surrounding the castle grounds. Beyond this oasis, the rest of the Autumn Highlands appeared gray and lifeless. A lot of rocky ground, buckled canyon-like passages, and distant fog. Even the moon didn't seem to shine as brightly here.

"I have no idea how long this'll take," I finally said. "But I kind of wish I'd brought Uriskel's pack out with us. I think I'm actually hungry."

"*Oh! He's hungry!*"

The distinctly female voice whispered through the air, apparently out of nowhere. It wasn't Sadie's voice, and she hadn't reacted. I frowned at her. "Did you hear that?"

She tensed immediately. "Hear what?"

"That voice. I said I was hungry, and—"

"*I want to feed him.*"

"*No, I do!*"

"Hey!" I scrambled to my feet, pulling the spelled dagger from my belt. Now there were two of them. "Who's there?"

Someone laughed. Two someones.

This time Sadie heard it too. She was up like a shot, trying to look everywhere at once. "What the hell?"

The air in front of us shimmered into two sparkling columns that solidified and became women.

"Jesus Christ," I breathed, ramming the knife back home. They were two of the mirror mender's attendants—nymphs, according to Uriskel. Both with waist-length blonde hair, delicate features, and ocean-blue eyes. One in a crimson red gown and the other in sheer, pale gold trimmed with blue. I tried not to notice how beautiful they were.

It wasn't easy. I almost felt compelled to notice.

They looked at each other, and the one in red said, "Who is Jesus Christ?"

"Never mind. Long story," I said. "What are you ladies doing out here, er...invisibly?"

"We're watching over you, of course." The one in gold looked insulted. "You are our noble guests."

"And we are your faithful servants, here to tend to your needs," the red-clad nymph said. "I am Treiya."

"And I am Fiorre. What is your name, noble sir?"

"Faithful servants?" I glanced at Sadie, and she shrugged. "Hate to tell you this, but I'm not noble," I said.

The nymphs smiled. "Of course you are noble," Treiya said. "You are the brother of Lord Taeral, son of Lord Daoin of the House of Ciar' Ansghar."

"Well, yeah. But...wait a minute," I said. "How did you know that?"

"Our mistress is wise and sees much," Fiorre said. "You are noble, and your companion is noble. A lady of the moon."

Sadie snorted. "Oh, yeah. I'm noble, all right."

"Anyway," I said, hoping we were done with the noble stuff. "I'm Gideon, and this is Sadie."

The nymphs curtsied. "It is an honor to meet you, Lord Gideon," Treiya said.

"And...Lady Sadie," Fiorre added with a giggle.

"*Mistress Sadie.*"

The new whisper-voice was male. A sparkling column appeared next to Sadie and became the former mannequin in the dark blue suit. He gave the nymphs a look of mild annoyance, and then turned to Sadie with a smile. "I am Vond, your faithful servant," he said as he took her hand and bowed to kiss her fingers. "Are you hungry as well, mistress? It would be my pleasure to feed you."

"I, er," Sadie stammered, her face flushing with color. "I guess?"

I dismissed a quick stab of jealousy. "Any more invisible people out here?" I said.

"Are we not sufficient?" Fiorre sniffed. With a narrow-eyed glance at Vond, she walked over and slipped her arm through mine. "We are here to please you."

"Yes," Treiya said, rushing to my other side. "Come, Lord Gideon. We will show you to the delights of the jade garden."

I couldn't do anything but let them lead me away.

The jade garden turned out to be one of the bigger ones close to the castle. A wooden lattice fence bursting with grape vines enclosed the area, where white stone paths wound among flower beds and small stands of mid-height fruit trees. Treiya and Fiorre brought me to a spacious arbor, with crystalline green climbing plants I couldn't identify growing up the supports and across the roof, and settled me on one of the cushioned benches on either side of the structure. Vond was right behind us, escorting Sadie to the opposite bench.

"Rest and enjoy yourself, Lord Gideon. We will return quickly to your side." Treiya grabbed Fiorre's hand and practically pulled her into the garden. "Hurry," she hissed. "Before Vond comes."

Vond watched them scurry off, and then lowered himself to one knee and kissed Sadie's hand again. "I shall return soon, Mistress Sadie," he said huskily. "Though I can hardly bear to lose the sight of you, even for a moment." He rose with a dazzling smile and walked after the nymphs.

"Whoa," Sadie said when they'd cleared out. "This is too weird."

"Tell me about it. I mean, Lord Gideon?" I said. "It was strange enough hearing 'Lord Taeral' in there."

She laughed. "Hey, at least you're not Lady Sadie."

"*Mistress* Sadie, if you please," I said. "You don't want to offend your faithful servant." I craned in the seat to look over the garden, and saw Treiya practically shove Vond away from a bunch of grapes he was trying to pick. "Any idea what the deal is here? These guys are falling over themselves playing who's-the-better-servant."

Sadie shook her head slowly. "Don't know much about nymphs," she said. "I thought they were all supposed to be female. And once Taeral said they..." She trailed off and cleared her throat deliberately. "He said they live to serve, they choose it. But basically everything they do is 'in pursuit of amorous liberties.' Pretty sure those were his exact words."

"Amorous liberties," I said. "That's an interesting way to put it."

Just then, Fiorre stepped back under the ardor with a whole harvest gathered in her skirt, and Treiya right behind her. They sat on either side of me and sent looks of smug triumph at Vond, who was a few steps back and carrying whatever he'd picked in his arms.

He ignored them and settled next to Sadie. "I hope these offerings please you, mistress," he said. "My own greatest pleasure is merely your smile bestowed upon me."

"Lord Gideon has no need for pretty, empty words," Treiya said loudly, reaching across me to pluck something from Fiorre's lap that looked like a miniature red pumpkin. She leaned in close and held it up with a seductive smile. "'Tis sweetness between his lips that will serve him best. Allow me but to feed you, my lord, and my gifts will slake your every hunger."

It dawned on me that outside the heavy-handed suggestion, she meant 'feed' literally. As in, she wanted to put food in my mouth.

"Er." I blinked at the little red pumpkin. "Hope you don't mind my asking, but...what is that?"

"Only the ripest of mallow fruit, of course." She rested a hand on my thigh and brushed the fruit against my lips. "I assure you, you'll find it quite delectable."

It was getting hard to think. So I let her feed me.

The mallow fruit was crisp and clean-tasting, sweet like honey with a hint of citrus. Much better than the mirror mender's tea. "It's very good," I said after I swallowed, to make sure I didn't hurt Treiya's feelings. "Thank you. I—"

"We are so pleased, Lord Gideon," Fiorre said, holding up something round and green. "Now, try this starling pear. It simply melts in your mouth."

I glanced frantically at Sadie. She'd already surrendered to Vond's ministrations, and sat looking awkward and bemused as he fed her a steady stream of grapes and berries.

I gave up and went with the flow.

Before long, I had to insist that I couldn't eat another bite. The nymphs looked disappointed, but they stopped putting things in my mouth, and I breathed a silent sigh of relief. Now I was a little thirsty—but I didn't dare ask for a drink.

If this was the kind of thing nobles usually did, I'd pass.

"So, what do you guys do when you're not...feeding visitors?" I said.

Treiya and Fiorre smiled at each other. "We also offer entertainment," Treiya said.

"Yes." Fiorre trailed her fingers down the front of my shirt, and I shivered hard. "Allow us to entertain you, Lord Gideon."

"And you as well, Mistress Sadie," Vond put in as he sidled closer.

I wasn't sure I wanted to take amorous liberties right now, and Sadie looked like she agreed with my sentiment. "Uh. Can we just..."

Suddenly, all three of them jumped up and gathered in a row at the back of the ardor, sending nervous glances at something in the garden.

It was Sharde.

"My mistress is ready to receive you," the massive man boomed as he glared at the nymphs. "If you'll kindly follow me."

Phew. Saved by the butler.

CHAPTER 32

When Sharde escorted us back to the parlor, I figured Taeral and Uriskel would be pretty much the way we left them. But they were already wearing their creations.

And they looked extremely royal.

Taeral had two arms again. The new prosthetic was carved with runes like the old one—but it was gold, and the hand I could see looked a lot more natural. No obvious clockwork. He wore a rich blue tunic belted at the waist over a black shirt with a high collar, tight pants the same shade as the tunic, and thigh-high black boots. A long black, hooded overcoat with flared sleeves completed the look.

She'd dressed Uriskel in blood red and black. His tunic was longer and sleeveless, with a double sash draped from the belt across his hips, and his boots had more straps than the ones I'd first seen him wearing. He wore black gloves to his elbows, the same style as the boots, and a hooded, flowing cape instead of a coat.

"Holy shit," Sadie said in a hushed tone. "You guys look terrifying."

The mirror mender, who stood beside her tea cart, flashed her eyes and made a slightly irritated sound.

"I mean that in a good way," Sadie said quickly. "This is amazing. I've never seen clothes like these...they're absolutely perfect for them."

"Aye, she's outdone herself," Taeral said, smiling as he walked toward us. "Wouldn't you say, Prince Uriskel?"

Uriskel held a gloved arm out and flexed a fist. "I suppose I cannot complain," he said. "For the price. And do not call me that, *Lord* Taeral."

"If you insist."

"MASTER GIDEON." The mirror mender clapped her hands, and a nymph rushed in from a doorway at the back of the parlor, pushing a blank-faced dressmaker's dummy. I assumed it was wearing my new clothes—black pants, black boots, a tastefully ruffled white shirt, and a three-quarter length black coat with a tapered waist. More elegant and expensive-looking than anything I'd worn in my life. "I DO HOPE YOU APPROVE," the mirror mender said.

"It's incredible," I said, and meant it. "Thank you."

The mirror mender bobbed her head and waved an arm. Suddenly the dummy was wearing my filthy, torn clothes, and I was wearing the suit.

Oh, man. I'd love to learn that trick.

"Exceptional," Taeral said. "It suits you, brother."

I gave a wry smile. "Guess I'll take your word for that."

"AND FOR YOU, MISTRESS SADIE." The mirror mender flashed and fluttered, like she was really excited about this one. "I HAVE CRAFTED YOU SUCH A WARDROBE, TO ACCENTUATE YOUR EXQUISITE BONE STRUCTURE AND PROVIDE THE IDEAL CHOICE OF GARMENT FOR EVERY OCCASION."

Sadie's brow furrowed. "Wardrobe?"

She clapped again. Another nymph scurried out with a fresh dressmaker's dummy. Which was completely naked, except for a strip of fabric around its throat.

The nymph removed the strip, walked over and handed it to Sadie with a dramatic flourish.

"Thank you," Sadie said carefully. "It's a...collar."

Okay, maybe the mirror mender was crazy. It was a pretty collar—deep green velvet, trimmed in black and adorned with clear, faceted crystals. An elegant hook and eye clasp with a short silver chain served to hold it closed.

But it wasn't a wardrobe. Not by any definition of the word.

"Perhaps if you tried it on," Taeral said, gently taking the collar from her hands.

"Yeah," she muttered. "Let's do that."

Standing behind her, Taeral draped it around her throat and connected the clasp. Then he smiled and stepped back.

Sadie's modern human clothes shivered and blurred, and became a silver-white, off-the-shoulder gown fit for a princess.

She drew in a sharp, surprised breath. "Oh! I don't..." she said, looking down at herself in sheer wonder. "Is this real?" she whispered.

"Real enough," Taeral said. "It is permanent glamour, and you can change it with a thought. Simply consider the type of garments you require, and the glamour will adjust to suit your needs."

"But I'm not Fae," she said uncertainly.

The mirror mender waved an arm. "YOU ARE A LADY OF THE MOON. AND THE MOON PROVIDES THE MAGIC."

"Um. Okay." Sadie bit her lip and looked at the ceiling a minute. "Say I wanted to wear something for...fighting."

The dress became a wrapped shirt with a bolo jacket, breeches and suede boots. And they looked just as beautiful on her.

"Oh my God." She glanced down, and then stared at the mirror mender with wide eyes. "I did something magic."

"Aye, you have," Taeral said. "It'll work even when you've...changed back. And those crystals are moonstone flecks, so you'll no longer need a luna-ball."

Sadie lifted a trembling smile. Her outfit flashed back to the princess gown, and she ran to the mirror mender and threw her arms around the floating torso. "I can't thank you enough," she said. "This is...just..."

The mirror mender's eyes glowed steadily. She ducked her head in approval and made a sound that was almost a purr. "YOU ARE MOST WELCOME, MISTRESS SADIE."

I couldn't help grinning. All this was definitely worth a lousy cup of tea.

——————◆——————

Much as I loved the new threads, I changed into my own human-realm clothes before we left the mirror mender's castle. Didn't want anything to happen to them, and we still had to take on the Unseelie Guard and the Queen.

Sharde showed us out to the courtyard and closed the big door firmly behind us. The place was already showing signs of reverting back to hibernation—castle walls yellowing, flag-stones buckling and separating, vines creeping around the statuary. "Does this place always curl up and die between guests?" I said.

"Aye. It's how she's served the Arcadian nobles as long as she has," Uriskel said. "She and her...attendants shut down completely when their services are not required. Only the troll remains alert, to wake the mirror mender once a visitor is approved for an audience."

"Troll?"

He nodded. "Sharde Switchback. He's served the mirror mender since her beginning."

"And when was that?" I said.

"Many thousands of years ago."

Damn. No wonder the guy was cranky—I'd hate everyone too, if I'd been awake for thousands of years.

"Hey. Lord Gideon." Sadie approached me with a smile. She'd changed back into her fighting outfit, and it was really hard not to notice the way the clothes clung to her. "I think I have something that belongs to you," she said, touching the pendant. "Now that I have my own moonstones, it's probably safe to take this off."

Taeral looked from her to me. "You gave her the moonstone?"

"Yeah," I said. "Because there's a super-charged full moon here. She went wolf when we crossed over, and it was the only way to keep her from changing. The stone absorbs moonlight."

He raised an eyebrow. "This was your idea, brother?" he said. "I am impressed."

"Thanks. I'm only an idiot half the time."

"Well, maybe less than half," Sadie said. "Anyway, you should have this back."

"Wait." Uriskel glanced at the sky and frowned. "Are you certain that's the best idea?" he said. "The stones on that collar are far smaller. They may not absorb enough light."

She gave him a wry smile. "Tell you what. If I go wolf, I promise to kill you last."

"I fail to be reassured by that," he muttered.

"Whatever. Here we go." She paused, and then took the pendant off.

Nothing happened.

"I guess you guys get to live today," she said as she handed me the moonstone. "See, that wasn't...oh. Oh, *crap.*" Her jaw clenched, and she closed her eyes tightly. "Jesus, I can really feel it now. The moon is so damned strong here."

I shoved the stone at her. "Take it back, quick."

"No. I'm okay." She opened her eyes and looked up with an expression of wonder. "I could change right now, if I wanted to," she said. "But I don't have to. I can control it. The collar's taking just enough light so the change isn't forced. And I bet it'll work like that back home, too. No more hiding from the full moon." A grin spread on her face. "I *love* this thing."

"I gotta say, it's pretty awesome." I put the pendant back on with a powerful feeling of relief I hadn't expected. I'd known it would be safe with her, but giving it up still hadn't felt right. There was probably only one person I could give the moonstone to without hesitation or concern.

I was the caretaker, but the stone belonged to Daoin.

183

"Well, I guess we're as ready as we're going to be," I said. I'd already told Taeral the short version of my visit with Nyantha, and he was glad I'd gone. Turned out that was who he'd planned to see about the DeathSpeaker stuff in the first place. "So, now what?"

"Now, we assault the palace," Uriskel said.

Taeral gaped at him "Excuse me?"

"I am a full royal. The portal works both ways—I can create one from here to either of the Courts," he said. "So we go to the palace and demand entrance. If we're denied, we defeat the Guard and enter anyway."

"That's your plan," Taeral said. "Defeat the Guard and storm the palace."

"You've a better one?"

"Aye, I do. *Any* plan but that one."

"Well, let's hear yours, then."

Taeral scowled. "At least let me attempt to contact Levoran," he said. "He may be able to help us get in without drawing the attention of the Guard."

"And if that fails?" Uriskel said.

He clenched a fist. "Then we fight."

CHAPTER 33

We emerged from the portal in a field of tall blue grass, like the stuff along the banks of the stream in the woods. In the near distance was a massive gate of black bars between two stone columns, with what looked like a single guard in front of it. And beyond the gate, at the top of a broad, gently rising hill, was the Unseelie palace set off against a backdrop of evergreens—the first of that type of tree I'd seen in Arcadia.

I squinted at the pale blue, glittering structure. "Is that castle made out of ice?"

"Celestine crystal," Uriskel said. "But yes, she'd meant it to be symbolic of the Winter Court. And she's quite vain as well. Pretty things appeal to her."

"Like my father," Taeral muttered under his breath. Louder, he said, "I cannot make out the guard at the gate from here. Whoever it is doesn't seem to have noticed us, or it may be Levoran. Though I doubt we'd be so lucky."

Uriskel narrowed his eyes at the gate. "What does this Levoran look like?"

"He is...well. Since my spark is recharged, it's simpler to show you." Taeral shimmered in place as his glamour shifted, and he became someone else.

Someone I recognized.

"I know him." My mind drifted back years, to a time I never liked to remember. I was fifteen when I'd met him, just the once—a massive, grizzled man with a scarred face, huge hands, and deep blue eyes. He never gave me his name, but he did give me something. "The moonstone," I said. "He's the one who brought it to me."

Taeral abruptly turned back into himself. "Levoran gave you the stone?"

"Yeah," I said. "I don't know how he found me or knew who I was, when *I* didn't even know…but that was him."

Taeral frowned slightly. "Daoin trusted him above all. I suppose if he were to leave it with someone, it would be Levoran. Though I'm not certain why—Moirehna always wanted the stone. It would've been easier if he'd brought it to the human realm in the first place." He turned to Uriskel. "Can you tell if it's him?"

"Of course not. I can see no better than you from here," Uriskel said. "But I'll find out."

With that, he jumped off the ground—and kept going up.

"Holy shit," Sadie said. "I guess he really can fly."

Taeral was too busy staring in shock to comment.

I looked at the gate again, and the lone figure in front of it. Something just didn't seem right. Why would there be only one guard? I didn't see anything at all moving between here and the palace. And if we could tell that was a person from this distance, shouldn't the guard be able to see there were people in the field? Especially considering the way we came in— through a big, glowing rip in the air.

I had a very bad feeling about this.

"Taeral," I said. "He should've seen the portal."

He tore his gaze from the sky and blinked at me. "What?"

"The guard. We came here in a big flash of light, remember?" I said. "And the guard didn't do anything. He's still just standing there."

"That is…unusual," he said as concern filtered into his face. "Perhaps we should—"

Sadie elbowed him and nodded up. "He's coming back."

Uriskel floated overhead and landed easily a few feet back from us. But there was nothing easy in his expression. "I've seen the guard," he said in rough, reluctant tones.

"Is it him? Levoran?" Taeral said.

"Aye, it is. But..." He shuddered visibly. "He's dead."

Jesus Christ. Well, that explained why he didn't move—but it was the most horrifying explanation I could imagine.

"No." Taeral backed up a step, shaking his head. "No, he cannot be. He is an Unseelie Guard," he said. "The Queen has never ordered one of her Guard killed, no matter what they've done."

"Well, she has now," Uriskel nearly shouted. "He's *dead*. She's had his corpse tied to the gate, and hung a blasted sign on him. He is—"

"*No*, he is not!" Lip curled in a snarl, Taeral half-turned and sprinted for the gate.

"Taeral!" Uriskel glared at his retreating back, then relaxed on a sigh and lowered his head briefly. "We'd better go after him, then," he said. "I'd not seen anyone else around out there...but that in itself is suspect."

I had to agree with that.

We didn't run as fast as Taeral, but we did pick up the pace. Just as we cleared the edge of the tall grass, Taeral wavered and fell to his knees beside the motionless figure. Sadie immediately broke into a run that faltered when she got close. But she went down in front of him, put her arms around him. And he embraced her back, his face contorted with grief and turned away from the gate.

The closer I got, the slower I moved. I could see Levoran clearly now—and I didn't want to.

There was blood everywhere. Coarse rope tied his wrists and ankles, his middle and his neck to the bars of the gate, like some gruesome scarecrow. His face was frozen in eternal agony. And a wooden plank had been nailed to the center of his chest. Wisps of smoke drifted from where the nails entered his body—they were cold iron, and he hadn't been dead long.

The runes burned into the plank read *traitor*.

187

"I may as well have killed him myself." Taeral struggled to his feet, with Sadie still supporting him. "If he hadn't helped me escape..."

"Then you would have died," Uriskel said firmly. "Along with your brother, your woman, and possibly your father."

No one corrected the 'your woman' part.

"He's sacrificed his life for his loyalty," Uriskel went on. "And it is a noble death. Now, only one question remains—will you honor his sacrifice and finish what you've come here to do, or wallow in your grief until you're captured and your friend has died in vain?"

Sadie looked like she wanted to punch him. But Taeral's features hardened, and he drew himself stiff. "I will *end* her," he growled.

"Better. Much better," Uriskel said. "And I truly hate to point this out, but...Levoran may still be able to help us." He looked at me. "Isn't that right, DeathSpeaker?"

Damn. Unfortunately, it was.

CHAPTER 34

For the first time, talking to the dead felt like a violation. Or maybe blasphemy.

It was partly because I knew what really happened when I did it now. I didn't want to drag this guy's soul out of wherever he was and shove him back into the land of the living to ask him a bunch of questions. He should be allowed to rest in peace.

But it had to be done. And at least I wouldn't have to hurt him. If he was a friend, he wouldn't struggle with trying to lie or resist answering.

"Okay." I let out an unsteady breath. "Taeral, this is gonna be…different, so try not to freak out," I said. "I learned a new way to do this."

He looked at me warily. "How different?"

"Extremely."

The first thing I did was to pry the sign carefully out of him. I couldn't stand it being there, still burning him, even if I wouldn't be able to see it with the glamour. Uriskel gave a nod of approval as I stepped back and threw the damned thing as far as I could.

I hardly had to think about reaching out, or pulling his soul in. It did get easier with practice. I only wished I didn't have to practice like this.

There was a sharp pain in my head, and a brief struggle. More surprise than resistance. I focused on the body, and almost instantly, the pressure left my head.

It appeared that the ropes and the blood vanished, and the corpse opened his eyes.

"Gods' blood," Taeral gasped. "Did you...bring him back?"

"It's a glamour," I said. "They were in my head before, when I talked to the dead. Nyantha taught me how to project them out."

"*Taeral. You've survived.*" The slightly transparent Levoran gave a confused smile. "*And I thought I had not. How am I here?*"

"He speaks?" Taeral blurted.

"*Apparently I do.*" Levoran looked at me. "*Ah, so that's how. You are the DeathSpeaker. And the young son of Lord Daoin. I remember you.*"

"I remember you, too," I said. "I'm so sorry you're...dead."

The apparition laughed. "*Now there's a phrase I'd never thought to hear spoken to me. One doesn't usually hear a thing, being dead.*"

"Levoran. We will avenge your death," Taeral said. "We're here to retrieve my father, and destroy Moirehna."

"*Is that your plan.*" His ghostly head turned to look at Sadie and Uriskel. "*A mistress of the moon, and the dark prince. Well. You've certainly a strong force...but I fear it may not be enough.*"

Uriskel frowned deeply. "I don't recall knowing you," he said. "How is it you know me?"

"*I've always had a gift for sensing the core of someone. It's how I knew you, young DeathSpeaker, when you'd not known yourself.*" His smile grew wistful. "*And how I knew you'd protect the stone. But now, you must return it to Lord Daoin— and do not let Moirehna know you have it.*"

I wasn't sure why, but I definitely wouldn't argue. I tucked the pendant inside my shirt. "Glad to, as long as we can get to him," I said. "Speaking of that. Do you have any idea how we can get into the palace?"

Levoran's brow furrowed. "*You've no need to compel me, DeathSpeaker. I'll answer freely.*"

"I didn't..." Oh, right. I'd asked him a question. "Sorry about that. I think it's just the way it works when I ask something. And, um—how did you not answer?"

"*Unfortunately, it's because I've no answer for you. There is no way,*" he said. "*None can enter the palace without the escort of a Guard. The spell is unbreakable.*" He shook his head sadly. "*If only I'd not died. I'd give my life all over again to serve the House of Ciar' Ansghar.*"

So we were totally screwed. Great.

"We fight, then," Uriskel said. "If we can force but one guard to yield—"

"*None will yield. Their loyalty is complete.*" Levoran's eyes burned red for an instant. "*They did not hesitate when she ordered them to execute me. My* brothers," he sneered. "*What I'd not give for a chance at retribution.*" He turned his gaze to me. "*DeathSpeaker. Can you not return my soul to my body, as Kelwyyn could?*"

The idea horrified me. Raising souls was one thing, but animating corpses? Desecration wasn't a strong enough word for that.

But he *really* wanted to fight. I could feel it burning his soul from the inside. And somehow I knew if he didn't get the chance, he'd spend the rest of his death feeling it. He'd never be at peace.

If there was any way I could help him, I had to. And if Kelwyyn had done it...maybe I could, too.

"I'm not sure," I finally said. "But I'll try."

"Gideon, are you mad?" Taeral hissed. "Why would you even attempt such a thing?"

"Because he wants to fight. And he deserves to."

Sadie nodded slowly. "Let him try. If it was me, I'd want him to."

"Aye. His will is strong, even in death," Uriskel said. "He'll not rest easy."

191

"Now that you've all spoken my mind for me." Levoran crooked a smile. *"For centuries I've remained by your father's side, young master Taeral. And I'll not desert him now, in his greatest hour of need. Even if I am dead."*

Taeral closed his eyes. "Very well. I understand."

"Okay," I said. "I've got this."

I hoped.

I could feel the invisible string connected me to Levoran's soul. Holding it was almost effortless, because he wasn't struggling to get away. I remembered Nyantha said that the dead could choose to be in the world of the living, like the banshees—and that if I let go of a soul, they'd either stay here, or return to the land of the dead.

But if I just released him, he'd be a soul floating around. I had to get him inside his body.

So maybe I could project him there.

I moved toward him. Direct contact always made things easier, and I didn't have time to practice this one. "I think I can push your soul into your head, and then let go," I said. "But I'm not sure if it'll stay there."

Levoran nodded gravely. *"Perhaps a binding spell,"* he said. *"I've the will to keep it there, once it's done."*

"It will not work," Taeral said. "The dead cannot be spelled."

"Except by the DeathSpeaker. He's done it once already, with the Redcap," Uriskel told him.

Taeral's brow lifted. "Is there anything you cannot do, brother?"

"Yeah. I can't cook, and I'm a lousy singer." I smirked and turned back to Levoran. "Well, here goes."

I had to reach up to lay a hand on his head. It was cold and stiff, like a hundred other corpses I'd touched. Shifting the glamour didn't seem like the best way to do this, so I figured I'd re-project him.

As I pulled the soul back into myself, the glamour vanished—and I was looking straight into the anguished features of the bloody corpse.

"*Don't let that trouble you, Gideon,*" Levoran said in my head. "*It was more fury than pain. The treacherous bastards.*"

I smiled in spite of the stabbing pain of his words. "I bet it was."

It was a lot harder forcing the soul through me, instead of out. The strain was physical and magical—I was sweating, trembling, and I could feel my spark drain. But I managed to guide it to the point of contact. There I pushed harder against what felt like solid marble, until I finally felt something pass out of me. So I let go of the remaining string.

The body jerked and thrummed beneath my hand.

A binding spell. The word came to me right away. "*Ceàngahlteh,*" I gasped.

And the corpse's actual eyes opened.

I staggered back and doubled over, trying to catch my breath. Damn, that took a lot out of me. I knew I'd never be able to do it in the human realm—there wasn't enough magic there. I could barely believe I'd done it here.

"Gideon!" Sadie rushed over and put an arm around my waist. "Are you okay? You're not bleeding are you?"

"No. I'm good. Just...tired." I shivered and drew myself straight.

Taeral and Uriskel were both staring at Levoran in open-mouthed shock.

Levoran shifted slightly. I could almost hear him creaking. "Perhaps someone could cut me down from here?" he said, in a voice like the wind rustling through dried leaves.

"Yes! Of course." Taeral shook himself and rushed over, reaching for his belt. Then he frowned. "Damn, I'd forgotten. The Guard took my dagger."

I handed him mine. "I think you should probably hurry," I said.

193

He nodded and started sawing through the ropes at his throat. "You're badly injured, Levoran," he said in choked tones. "Should we...heal you?"

"I'd not try that. Besides, I can't feel a thing. Being dead seems to have its advantages." Levoran's mouth lifted, a stiff grimace that was probably supposed to be a smile. "Thank you for this, young DeathSpeaker," he said. "I'll not be able to repay you."

"You already have," I said.

Taeral cut the last of the ropes, tossed the dagger back to me, and caught Levoran as he pitched forward. After a minute, the dead man gestured him away and stood on his own. "All seems to be in order. Well, save that I'm dead," he said. "Now, we've a palace to storm."

"I'm afraid I'll not let that happen, Brother Levoran."

The cold voice came from the other side of the gate. It belonged to the Guard who'd stabbed me back at the Castle, the one with dark brown braids, golden eyes, and thorns tattooed on his face. He still wore armor that seemed to be made out of light, and now he had two swords hanging from his belt, in addition to the spelled dagger.

And he hadn't come alone.

CHAPTER 35

Levoran whirled to face the Guard. "Aonghas," he spat in his dead-leaves voice. "I've a score to settle with you, *Captain.*"

Oh, good. This guy was Daoin's replacement.

"Correct me if I'm wrong, Levoran, but haven't I killed you once?" His grin was just as cold as his voice, but the half-dozen other Guards behind him weren't smiling at all. "I'll gladly do it again," he said. "And it seems I've you to thank for this opportunity... DeathSpeaker." He turned his gold gaze to me. "*Amaedahn, naech crohgaa.*"

This time I understood the words. Foolish, but brave.

"Yeah, that's me," I said. "How about you surrender, so we don't have to kill you?"

Aonghas laughed. "Oh, I like you. Such spirit," he said. "Barely on his feet, and telling *me* to surrender. It's a shame I'll have to turn you over to her Majesty." He moved forward and leaned an arm casually against the gate. "I'll make you a deal, then, since she only wants you. Turn yourself in, and we'll let your friends live. All but Levoran." He sent a heated glare at the walking corpse. "Him, I'll have to teach a lesson in *staying* dead when I kill him."

"That's quite a deal," I said. "Let me think about it. No."

"Suit yourself. One way or another, you'll be going to the Queen."

I flashed a cold smile of my own. "Well, you're right about that."

"So it's to be a battle. This pleases me." Aonghas stepped back and drew one of his swords. "*Oscaihl'te.*"

The gate swung open.

I glanced back. Taeral stood with his metal arm raised, and Uriskel had a playing card in his hand. Sadie was already halfway to wolf. Levoran just looked huge and furious, and I still held the dagger.

This was going to happen fast.

"That's *my* weapon, you pompous snake," Levoran snarled. "*Tuariis'caen.*"

The sword wrenched itself from Aonghas' hand and flew into Levoran's.

I decided now was a good time to attack.

I lunged at the Unseelie captain, wrapping him in a bearhug so he couldn't draw another weapon. From the corners of my eyes, I saw a rush of motion—Uriskel taking to the air, full-wolf Sadie springing with bared fangs, Taeral throwing a gesture that seemed to spit out a wave of magic. Then we hit the ground, and the impact slammed through me.

I lifted the dagger and swung for his throat, but my awkward aim was off. The blade glanced off the light-armor with a resounding clang.

Aonghas grinned. "*Leíchtraana.*"

An electric shock blasted through me and sent me flying.

I came down hard and tumbled once. By the time I struggled to my feet, Levoran was charging Aonghas, sword raised. The captain pulled the other sword and managed to meet his blow.

Sadie had one of the guards down, her teeth snapping for his throat. Taeral had wrestled a dagger from another and fought him hand-to-hand. One guard lay motionless on the ground, his body smoldering—from Uriskel's card spell, I guessed.

And one was headed straight for me, wielding a long, broad two-handed sword.

My dagger wasn't going to cut it against that.

He swung, and I managed to duck under the blow. Momentum carried him past me. I held out a hand and shouted, "*Dei'ahmael!*"

His sword clattered to the ground. He snarled and spat the word back at me, and the dagger dropped.

"*Tuariis'caen,*" we both said at the same time. The weapons returned.

Okay, so weapon spells were out.

He rushed me again, the massive sword upraised. I gestured and said, "*À dionadth.*" This time I felt something in me strain as I cast the spell—my spark was draining. And the moon, strong as it was, couldn't charge it back fast enough.

The sword clanged against the shield...and shattered it. And the guard drew back for another blow.

"Too simple, halfling," he sneered as he advanced. "Had you thought yourself equal to the Unseelie Guard? With your weak human half, you're no match for a true Fae."

Huh. Too simple...or not simple enough?

I smiled. "*Beith na cohdal.*"

And I thoroughly enjoyed the look on his face as he staggered and slumped into sleep.

But now I really had nothing left. I clutched the dagger tightly and looked around, trying to assess the tide of the battle. Levoran and Aonghas were still swinging away at each other, but Aonghas was losing ground. A third guard lay prostrate with blood splashed on his armor. Taeral had just brought one down and charged another, screaming and waving a bloodied dagger in the air like a flag.

There was a sound behind me. I turned to find a guard rushing me, a knife in one hand and the other outstretched to cast a spell.

Well, at least he probably wouldn't kill me. The Queen wanted to do that.

197

Before he reached me, Uriskel dropped from the sky like a stone. He snatched the guard by the wrist and carried him straight up. "Sadie," he shouted. "Fetch."

He let go, and Sadie lunged out of nowhere in a graceful arc to collide with the falling Unseelie and slam him to the ground.

I couldn't help a tired laugh. She'd make him pay for that fetch comment later.

Taeral and Uriskel together brought the sixth guard down. Now only Aonghas remained—but he clearly wasn't going to come out on top. His light-armor had vanished, and he was panting and bleeding, just barely fending off Levoran's hammering blows.

I made my way toward the fight. "Hey," I called. "Maybe he wants to surrender now."

Aonghas glanced at me with fiercely sparking eyes. And Levoran drove the sword through his stomach.

He gasped and fell to his knees. It was an obvious effort for him to lift his head, and he looked around as everyone still standing drifted over.

None of them were his men.

"Well met, Levoran," Aonghas said. He winced and wiped dripping blood from his mouth with the side of his fist. "I am honored to die in battle at your hands."

"An honor you did not afford me, Aonghas, and one I'll not grant you." Levoran reached down, gripped the sword and pulled it free, producing a pained cry from the captain. "You will live to suffer her punishment for your failure."

With that, he reversed the sword and smashed the club-like hilt into Aonghas' temple. The Unseelie's eyes rolled to white, and he pitched forward.

"That was immensely satisfying." Levoran grinned. "On to the palace, then?" he said.

"That is the plan," Taeral said, turning to Uriskel with a smile. "Defeat the Guard and storm the palace."

"Aye. And it's a good plan," he said.

Sadie, who'd changed back to a person in fighting clothes, punched him in the arm. "Except for the fetch part, you asshole."

He shrugged. "You did respond to the command."

She rolled her eyes and gave a half-smile. "Whatever. Let's go."

I couldn't believe we'd won. But we still had to face the Queen—and my magic was just about spent. I didn't know about the rest of them, but none of us had escaped the fight unscathed. We were all bleeding and exhausted despite the triumphant mood. And Levoran was literally dead.

This part of the plan might not go so well.

CHAPTER 36

Up close, the Unseelie palace was an incredible sight.

It wasn't just ice blue. Translucent, shimmering bands of purple, green and pink rippled just beneath the surface of the crystals that rose in formation to create turrets and towers. The moon's light refracted endlessly on itself among the faceted crystal, creating the illusion that the whole palace was moving.

The post-battle silence held as we approached the massive double doors, made of an iridescent jet-black material that could've been crystal or stone. I still didn't like it—I half believed there were twice as many guards waiting on the other side of those doors. But Levoran didn't seem concerned.

Then again, he actually enjoyed fighting.

The dead guard reached the palace first. He pressed a hand against the doors, and said, "*Beilách.*"

I tensed as they swung open slowly, and didn't breathe until no one attacked us.

Levoran stepped onto the threshold and stood aside. "Come in," he said. "You are welcome in this place."

I wasn't sure I felt welcome. But I filed inside with the others, and stopped to stare as the doors closed behind us. The interior was just as breathtaking—all ice blue and jet black crystals, with shifting iridescence that rippled through the deserted great room we stood in. It was like being underwater in a pristine blue ocean.

"We'll likely find her in the throne room," Uriskel said. "We will confront her, and demand the return of Daoin and Reun."

Levoran laughed softly. "It's as good a plan as any. And it worked so well the last time," he said. "Still, I suspect there's a chance she may not cave to your demands."

"We'll figure something out," I said, not believing a word of it. But we didn't have too many options, and Levoran was right. It was as good a plan as any.

And Uriskel might just have a trump card—if he got the opportunity to play it.

Levoran took the lead toward the back of the huge crystal room, and Taeral rushed a little to catch up with him. "Any idea what she's done to Daoin?" he said. "I know she's taken him to her chambers, but nothing beyond that."

"Whatever she's done, she'd not shared it with me or any other Guard. At least, before she ordered me killed." Levoran's jaw clenched. "Considering the state he was in when they brought him through...well, it's just one more reason to make her pay." He glanced at Taeral with a stiff expression. "What happened to him?" he said softly. "I never had the opportunity to ask."

Taeral stared straight ahead. "A group of humans captured him. Tortured him for twenty-six years," he said. "He's no memory of anything before the moment we rescued him. He barely recalls I'm his son, and he's just learned that Gideon is as well."

"*Humans* did that to him?"

"For the most part. A *baughan* accomplished the rest."

Bogeyman. I hadn't thought about Murdoch in a while— but he'd saved Taeral's life, and Daoin's, when he used sheer terror to burn the Milus Dei programming out of Daoin's mind. Along with several years of his life.

We could've used him on this mission. But he'd gone off to do whatever bogeymen did when they weren't reluctantly fighting evil cults.

Levoran led us into a corridor like a crystal throat. It branched into a Y at the far end, and he took the right-hand path. "Be ready," he said. "The throne room's just ahead."

I didn't think I'd ever be ready. But at least I could sense a little of my spark restored.

Enough for just one spell.

Another black crystal door stood at the end of the corridor. Levoran placed a hand on it and looked back. "Anyone care to surrender now?" he said. "No? All right, then." He pushed the door open.

The space beyond it was completely dark.

"Let me guess," Sadie muttered. "That's not suspicious, either."

"Oh, it's highly suspect," Levoran said cheerfully. "But here we are, so we may as well go inside. I'm certain someone can light the place up."

We filed in one by one, with Levoran holding the door. Just as he closed it behind us, a blinding flash of pure gold light consumed the space—and a female voice thundered, "*Gaich seabh'fos!*"

And I couldn't move a single muscle.

CHAPTER 37

The dazzling light was slow to fade. When it finally did, everything in me clenched like a fist. This was definitely the throne room—and it was not a pleasant place. There were no crystals here. Everything was black marble and burnished gold.

And the walls were made of mirrors.

The room was an octagon...maybe. It was almost impossible to tell for sure, because the vast, angled mirrors of the walls were pristine and gleaming, catching a hundred reflections and echoing them back into infinity. My eyes watered and my head spun sickly as I tried to adjust to the visual assault.

For some reason it was especially painful to look straight across the room at the raised platform where the thrones probably were.

But it hurt just as much tracking my gaze slightly to the left, past the platform, and seeing Reun.

His glamour was gone. I'd never seen his true form—pale green skin, hair that would've been golden blond without the filth and blood matted into it. The only clothing he had on was a string tied around his waist, with leather panels at the front and back. There were gold bracelets clamped midway around his upper arms, and a gold collar around his throat. He was battered and unconscious, maybe even dead, on his knees with his arms suspended and chained to the mirror wall behind him.

I would've shuddered if I could move. Instead I focused straight ahead, trying to will myself to see what was there. I made out two thick, freestanding stone columns at either side of the platform, and an empty throne that was constructed with bones. Thick black velvet drapes hung behind the platform, interrupting the endless reflection.

Finally, I managed to see the second throne beside the empty one, and the Unseelie Queen sitting in it.

Beautiful didn't do her justice.

Her hair was the color of flames, her skin like golden sun. Intensely green eyes, the exact same shade as Uriskel's, pink and perfect bow lips flirting with the smallest of smiles. Poets would've committed suicide trying write about her face, because words fell so far from sufficient to describe it. Her flowing gown was whiter than fresh snow.

I hated her. And I still wanted to fall at her feet and worship her.

She rose from the throne with movements that put grace to shame, and practically floated across the platform. "I sense your concern. Your Seelie friend lives, dear ones," she said. "My courtesans have merely exhausted him for the moment."

Angels wept when she spoke. And I wanted to rip her tongue out.

"Have you nothing to say for yourselves?" she said, and smiled sweetly. "Oh, yes. How rude of me...you cannot speak."

"I've something to say, Highness."

Levoran. A sliver of relief lodged in me—maybe we still had a chance. Her magic wouldn't work on him.

I just hoped her charms didn't, either.

Her exquisite face relaxed in shock as Levoran moved toward her. "Impossible," she said in a commanding tone. "I personally watched you die, traitor. *Miilé lahn!*"

The translation sickened me. A thousand knives.

But Levoran kept coming.

"Don't you know, Highness?" he said as he reached the steps of the platform. "Only the DeathSpeaker can compel the dead."

"DeathSpeaker," she whispered, her green gaze darting to me. "Can it be true?"

Levoran grinned a horrible grin. "Your eyes cannot lie, Highness. Neither can my soul—and it wants revenge."

He lunged at her.

She vanished, and reappeared between the two thrones.

"Why, Levoran," she said with a wicked smile. "I believe you mean to harm me. Guard!"

"Your Guard is lying down on the job," he said.

Her smile broadened. "Not all of them. My most loyal remains by my side, always."

The black curtains parted, and a figure strode out dressed in the uniform of the Guard—armor of light, sword and dagger, a jeweled band on his brow. Long black hair like a curtain of silk, vivid blue eyes. Sculpted from muscle and fury.

Twin curved scars along either side of his face.

Levoran gasped. "Lord Daoin!"

Without a word, Daoin drew his sword and charged.

———————◗◉◖———————

The struggle was short-lived.

Levoran was too stunned, and too loyal, to put up much of a fight. He didn't even touch his sword. When Daoin swung at him, he leaned out of the way and made a half-hearted attempt to shove him.

Daoin shoved back. And though Levoran was nearly twice his size, he shouldered him to the ground. Then he grabbed the dead guard one-handed, flung him back-first against one of the stone columns—and drove the sword through both him and the column with a horrible grinding sound. Sparks showered to the floor behind him as metal screamed through stone.

"I'm all right," Levoran gasped, waving a dismissive hand. "Still dead."

He shuddered, and his head rolled forward bonelessly.

Daoin trained a flat blue gaze on him. "Shall I finish him, Highness?" he said in a deep, rich voice that was nothing like the Daoin I knew.

"No, *gallae*. You've done well…you have pleased me," she said. "Leave him for now and come to me."

My mind refused to understand the word she called him, *gallae*. The closest I could get was *my sweet bitch.*

Some term of endearment.

"Of course. I live to please you, Moirehna." His eyes softened as he looked at her. If he was under some kind of spell, it was an extremely natural one—because he seemed happy, almost proud to do as she told him. He mounted the platform, went to her side and looked out across the room. "What of these others?" he said. "Are they a threat to you?"

His cold stare held absolutely no recognition. He didn't know us—any of us.

Without even seeing him, I could feel Taeral's pain.

"Not particularly," the Queen said. "But there is one I'd like you to…deal with."

She gestured at me, an impatient flick of her wrist. And I could move again.

"What the hell did you do to him?" I had to forcibly restrain myself from trying a spell. I only had one in me, and something told me it would be wasted on her. The power rolled from her in waves, bright as a beacon.

Whatever I did with my last bit of magic, I had to make it count.

She laughed. I shook my head, trying to dislodge the sound from my brain—it was enthralling, pure as silver bells. "Why, I've restored his memories," she said. "For the most part. At least those of the years before he had such determined, foolishly daring sons. A time when his loyalties lay only with me, his Queen." Her smile was lethal. "And I'll restore the rest…after he's killed you, and your oh-so-noble brother. So that he must live with the knowledge of exactly what he's done."

Jesus Christ. There was no way I could take Daoin—not like this, with his magic and physical strength intact. He'd been a feared warrior in Arcadia for centuries, and I had zero chance against him. But maybe I could keep the Queen talking until I figured something out.

"So you can only have his loyalty through magic," I said. "Isn't that kind of a letdown?"

Daoin snarled and went for his sword, but she held him back with a touch. "Surely you do not think *you* can rattle me," she said. "You, the whelp of that filthy human whore who stole him from me. And you are the DeathSpeaker as well." She walked forward a few steps. "That alone merits your death sentence, before you become too powerful. If that is possible with human blood in your veins."

"Maybe I'm already too powerful." I jerked forward, like I was going to attack.

In a single, lightning move, Daoin jumped from the platform to land at the bottom of the stairs with his sword drawn. He glowed with a threatening black light. "Move again, foul halfling spawn, and I'll lay you open and strike you dead before your guts hit the floor."

And I thought Uriskel was terrifying. At full power, Daoin made him look like a newborn puppy.

"It delights me so to hear you say such things," the Queen trilled. "But take your time, *gallae*. Kill him slowly. I wish to savor his anguish, like the finest of sweet wine."

Daion gave a frosted smile, colder than deep winter. "It will be my pleasure, Highness."

"Wait!" Desperation sparked an insane idea that would probably make things worse—but it was my only play. Levoran said the Queen wanted the moonstone.

So I'd give it to her…and hope like hell she commanded her loyal Guard to deliver it.

An expression of bemused impatience crossed her face. "The worm wishes to speak?" she said. "Choose your words carefully, whelp. They will be your last before you scream."

Right. No pressure. "You like loyalty, right?" I said. "Well, I like being alive. So I'll swear loyalty to you, in exchange for my life. I even have a gift to prove my devotion."

I tried not to think about how the others were feeling right now. They could still hear, and they probably wanted to kill me. For a few seconds, I was uncomfortably grateful that they couldn't move or speak—because they'd ruin any miniscule chance I had.

Her perfect lip curled in disdain. "You've nothing I want, halfling brat."

"Oh, I think I do." I pulled the pendant out of my shirt. "How about this?"

Her eyes grew impossibly wide. "The master stone," she breathed. "How did *you* lay hand to that?"

"Doesn't matter. I have it." *Master stone*? I couldn't even begin to figure out what that meant. But I knew one thing—the first time Daoin touched it after we brought him out of Milus Dei, he'd remembered something important.

He remembered that Taeral was his son.

I only hoped it would work again.

The Queen smiled. "Yes. I will have the stone," she said. "Bring it to me at once, *gallae*."

Perfect.

I slipped the cord over my head. As Daoin approached with an outstretched hand, I slapped the stone into it—and before he could react, squeezed his fist around it. "*Cuimmáihg*," I said with all my remaining strength.

Remember.

Daoin went rigid. Clean, blue-white light poured from his fist, bathing the entire room in its glow. He shuddered, stumbled back and dropped to one knee, his mouth open in a silent scream.

"What have you done?" the Queen cried. "You weak, miserable abomination! *What have you done to my love?*"

The light turned off, like a switch being thrown. And Daoin rose slowly, with sheer rage etched into every line of him. He turned to face the Queen in stiff, stilted jerks—like he was almost too angry to move.

"You do not love. Highness." He raised the pendant in front of him. "*Calhaiom'nae solaas geahlí!*"

My mind whispered a translation. Sword of moonlight.

The moonstone flashed a concentrated burst of light that solidified into a gleaming blue-white blade with a simple hilt. Daoin gripped the sword and reached the platform in a fluid leap, the light of his weapon leaving an ethereal trail in the air behind him.

He drove it into the Queen, just below her ribcage.

Her anguished cry was piercing enough to shatter glass. The force of the blow slammed her into the throne, and he shoved the sword all the way through until the end jutted between the bones of the throne, dripping with blood. A crimson stain bloomed on her white gown and spread quickly.

Daoin wasn't even breathing hard. "You killed the mother of one son, and exiled the other to her death. You murdered my oldest, most loyal friend. And you'd have had me slaughter my own sons," he rasped. "I will not only destroy you. I will destroy the very idea of you, and Arcadia will never recall your existence."

With that he stepped back and drew his dagger, preparing to follow through on his threat.

CHAPTER 38

"Stay your hand, Lord Daoin."

The voice was Uriskel's. I half-turned to find the rest of them free or moving—Levoran starting to stir, Sadie shivering and looking everywhere at once, and Taeral already headed for the platform. He didn't even seem to have heard what Uriskel said.

But Daoin did.

"I know you," he said. "The puppet of the Seelie Court. And I've no idea what you're doing here, but this is not your concern."

The only sign that the insult bothered him was a slight twitch in his jaw. "It is very much my concern." He started toward them, pulling his deck of cards as he walked.

I grabbed his arm. "Don't."

He paused to glare at me, then shrugged me off and kept walking.

I had to assume he knew what he was doing—and I should probably stay out of all this, anyway. So I went to Sadie, who grabbed my arm frantically and whispered, "I don't know what to do first. They're going to kill each other...and look at Reun, and Levoran..."

"I think we should probably wait," I said. "Just a minute, maybe."

She looked unconvinced, but she calmed down a little.

Taeral reached the platform first. "Father," he said, like he barely dared to breathe. "Are you truly restored?"

He faced him with a genuine smile. "Aye. And once I've seen this wicked wraith destroyed, we will rejoice together."

"Why wait? Allow me to join you in her destruction."

"My son." Daoin clapped him on the shoulder.

Behind them, the Queen stirred and moaned on her bloody throne. Her eyes opened, glittering with wicked intent, and she raised a slender hand.

Uriskel ran onto the platform and threw one of his cards at her. "*Dhuunad sios'na draíohtae!*"

The card traveled like a rock. It struck her square in the chest and burst into smoke on impact.

And her glamour fell away instantly.

Her skin was true gold, gleaming like metal and tinged with a blush of blue. Delicate pointed ears, hair like blood-red vines with curling, feathered wisps that looked like leaves. Her narrow, heart-shaped face took on harsh angles and shadows, reflecting a promise of cruelty. And her long, triple-jointed fingers ended in sharpened ivory claws. Still beautiful, but in a predatory way—like a tiger, built to kill.

She gritted her teeth and gestured at Uriskel. "*Míilé lahn.*"

He failed to be struck by a thousand knives.

He approached her with an awful grin. As Daoin and Taeral looked on in shock, he grabbed the hilt of the moon sword, pulled it free with a grisly tearing sound, and handed it back to its owner. "Your weapon, Lord Daoin," he said.

Daoin accepted it slowly. "*Tuariis,*" he said without taking his eyes from Uriskel. The sword collapsed into a pendant again.

"This cannot be," the Queen gasped. She tried to rise, and fell back on the throne. "Only a full royal can strip another Fae's magic."

I'd heard that exact sentence before somewhere. Gee, I wondered where.

"Well, then. I must be a full royal," Uriskel drawled. "Do you not recognize me, Mother?"

211

She shuddered and blanched almost as white as her gown. "Uriskel," she said unevenly.

"Aye. The child you cast off to die...and now, the only heir to your throne." He took a step forward. "You ignored my existence and left me at the hands of my father. For two centuries. Have you any *idea* what cruelties the Seelie Court is capable of?" he spat. "Compared to them, your idea of torture is a pleasant massage." His face twisted in disgust. "A thousand knives. Really. Can you do no better than that? *Highness?*"

Taeral and Daoin glanced at each other, and backed slowly down the platform steps.

"You cannot destroy me," the Queen rasped. "I am your blood. Your mother."

Uriskel laughed. The absolute contempt in that sound made my skin crawl. "Perhaps Daoin could not destroy you completely, though his will might have given him the edge he'd need. But do not doubt that I could, if I so chose," he said. "I'll not do so now, but only because I've a worse fate in mind for you."

She stared at him. "What might that be?"

"You will live, knowing that you can never touch those you've tried the hardest to tear down," he said. "You will swear an oath, a binding promise never to harm nor command harm to my family and loved ones, nor Lord Daoin's family and loved ones. Nor the Seelie noble." He paused and clenched a tight fist. "Regarding him, you will restore his magic. You will clothe him. And you'll erase the memories of every miserable courtesan who's violated him—and his own as well, if he so chooses."

Something terrible in his voice suggested that he'd been through what Reun had.

"And if I do not?" she said.

"Then I will destroy you. And with the backing of my brother, I will take your pathetic throne, and shred every wicked value of your rule."

"Your brother," she said flatly. "Who is..."

"Braelan. King of the Summer Court."

The Queen shivered and closed her eyes. "Very well," she whispered. "Restore me, and it shall be done."

"Swear it first. And then I will restore you."

She sent him a hateful glare. "I should not be surprised that my son is twisted as me."

"Oh no, Highness. I'm far more twisted than you." His awful grin returned. "Now—"

"Uriskel, wait," I said, remembering when I'd asked Taeral if there was any way to cancel his promise. A royal pardon—something he insisted he'd never get. But right now we had the Unseelie Queen doing whatever we wanted. "I want her to pardon Taeral."

Taeral shot a glare at me. "Gideon, what are you talking about?"

"Your promise to protect me." I moved toward him. "You don't need it," I said. "I already know you'll do everything you can to keep me safe. And I can't stand knowing you'll die if something does go wrong."

His angry expression melted into something else. "And you claimed not to be noble," he said roughly. "Very well. But I'll hold myself to that promise, consequences or not."

"Yeah, I know. That's why you deserve to be free of it."

Uriskel cleared his throat. "Are we finished? I've a wicked wraith to ruin here, if you'd not mind terribly."

I grinned. "Ruin away."

"Thank you." He turned back to the Queen. "Now, swear it. All of it, including Lord Gideon's request. And you will speak every one of their names, so there's no chance of you weaseling out of your promise."

With a baleful expression, she started talking.

It was a long list.

Daoin watched for a moment, and then gripped Taeral wordlessly and headed for Levoran, who was at least conscious now—but still dead, and fading fast. "My dear friend," he said heavily. "Let me help you down."

As he pulled the sword out, Levoran released a bark of air. "Do not be troubled, Lord," he said as he slid down the stone column. "I cannot feel it."

"And yet I feel you slipping." Daoin crouched in front of him. "Let us speak of better times, while we still can."

Levoran nodded carefully. Somehow, there were tears in his dead eyes.

I looked away and found Taeral approaching Sadie and me. "It seems this promise will take some time," he said. "I've a bit of spark remaining. Why don't we go and release Reun from his bonds, at the least?"

That sounded like a great idea to me.

CHAPTER 39

Outside the Unseelie palace, the moon blazed down on pristine silence. But this time, it didn't feel threatening.

We made our way to the gate without speaking, all of us whole and recovering—except Levoran. He stumbled along stiffly with Daoin and Taeral on either side of him for support. The binding spell was failing, because his body was in worse shape than before.

And because he'd lost the will to keep it. He'd accomplished what he returned for.

Beyond the gate, we headed for a clearing around a large, leafless tree, just outside the field of blue grass. Father and son settled Levoran at the base of the tree, and he leaned back against it with a sigh.

"I shall miss this realm," he said softly. "There is no moon where I'm going. But...there are stars. So many of them." One corner of his mouth lifted. "I could spend five lifetimes counting them and not be done with it. And now I've more time than that. Eternities of it. So I believe that is what I'll do...rest, and count the stars."

Daoin knelt and took his hand. "There are no words, save these," he said. "*Is féider leis an éirí an bóthar leat.*"

"Aye. And someday far from now, may we meet again upon that road, my friend." Levoran smiled, and his eyelids drooped down. He struggled to force them open. "DeathSpeaker...Gideon," he slurred. "Perhaps you'd be so kind as to release me."

I couldn't speak. Instead I went to him and knelt at his other side, where I finally found the right words. "It would be my honor."

He nodded, and his eyes fluttered closed again.

I knew it would be easier sending his soul back where it was trying to go, and it was. I laid a hand on his forehead, and his soul flowed into me. Within seconds I felt him in my head—and heard his voice, one last time.

Should you ever need me, Lord Gideon, you've but to call. I will always answer.

I smiled. "Thank you," I said. "But I'll try to leave you to your rest, and your stars."

And I released him.

———————◆———————

Daoin had insisted on burying Levoran immediately, and alone. No one had tried to stop him when he took hold of the body and vanished with it.

Now the rest of us sat on the ground in a rough circle, letting the tension wear off as we waited for him. At the moment, most of my worry was for Reun. He'd accepted the clothes the Unseelie Queen gave him—winter blue pants and tunic, black boots, and a black coat. But he refused to have the memories of what happened to him erased.

He said he'd lost enough when his wife took the better part of four centuries from him before she died, and he wanted to keep what was left intact.

Still, he hadn't said a word since we left the palace.

Just when I decided to try talking to him, to make sure he was still in there, Reun stirred and looked around. "Well, I must say I regret missing your victory over Moirehna," he said. "Tell me...how did you defeat her?"

Uriskel flashed a smile. "With the ace of diamonds."

"The what, now?"

"Long story," I said. "Reun, are you sure you're okay? I mean..." I didn't want to elaborate. I couldn't imagine what he'd been through, but I knew it was brutal.

"Aye. At least, I will be." A distant expression came over him, and a moment later he shook it away. "I am...humbled," he said. "It's an experience I'd not want to repeat. But I will not forget. Taking advantage of the powerless—nearly every noble has been guilty of this to some degree, including myself. Now I know exactly how devastating the receiving end can be." His eyes gleamed briefly with rage. "And I will never engage in such behavior again."

"Reun. You've no need to punish yourself this way," Taeral said. "You are no longer who you were. You've proven that many times over."

He nodded faintly. "Thank you. That means much to me, after what I've done to you," he said. "But I'll keep my pain, as you keep yours. And perhaps it will serve us both someday."

"I can attest that it will," Uriskel said. "Obviously."

Sadie smirked. "Two hundred years and a deck of cards, and you can be a badass, too."

"Aye, perhaps. But you'll never equal me."

"Have I mentioned how refreshingly modest you are?" She smiled—but then her gaze focused on something beyond him, in the grassy field, and her face fell. "Oh, shit," she said. "What is *that?* Please tell me it's not sprites."

A primal alert raced through me as I followed her stare and saw the distant cloud of motion rising from the grass. Heading straight for us.

But something was different. The sprites were a gray mass of buzzing malevolence, and this cloud was a riot of colors and whispers and tiny flashes of light. The colors grew brighter as the cloud moved in.

"They're not sprites," Uriskel whispered reverently.

Taeral and Reun sat up straighter. "I've not seen so many in decades," Taeral said, in the same awed tone.

"So many what?" I said. "Do they have teeth?"

Reun smiled. "They'll not harm you."

My pounding heart eased, and then stopped in breathless wonder as the cloud engulfed us.

Butterflies.

I'd never seen one so big, let alone hundreds. Or maybe thousands. Their wingspans ranged from six inches to a full foot or more, and they were every vivid, brilliant color imaginable—delicate jeweled wings, swirled and spotted with a rainbow of beauty. They fluttered gently, almost curiously around us, alighting for brief seconds on the ground, or a leg, or the top of a head.

I didn't dare breathe. It was the most incredible sight I'd ever experienced, and I didn't want it to end.

Sadie lifted a trembling hand, and a butterfly landed on her outstretched fingers. One of the larger ones, with wings of dappled crimson and sun-bright yellow. There was a glowing white spot on its back like a small, cold flame.

She drew her arm in slowly. The butterfly stayed in place, its wings wafting up and down like slow breaths. When it was close to her face, her eyes filled with startled tears. "It's a person," she whispered. "The glowing thing. There's a tiny person riding the butterfly."

"Aye. They'd be pixies." Uriskel crooked an arm, and two vibrant purple butterflies with glittering silver-trimmed wings landed there in near-perfect unison. "They sow magic throughout the realms, much as your bees spread pollen."

My throat clenched in sheer wonder. So there were some beautiful things in Arcadia, after all.

I held a hand out the way Sadie had, and one of the butterflies alit almost instantly. It was big, about a foot and a half from wingtip to wingtip, but it weighed almost nothing. Its wings were sapphire blue and emerald green, each with a coin-sized spot of gold in the top center like blind eyes. The small white flame sat just above the wings.

"Hello, there," I whispered, drawing the butterfly closer until I could make out the pixie. It *was* a tiny person, about an inch tall, vaguely female and wreathed in flickering light—and with wings of her own. Six slender, teardrop-shaped wings arranged in three pairs. The top two overlapped and curved up, while the lower pair curved down.

The pixie made a musical sound, like chimes on the wind. Suddenly she lifted from her mount and hovered in front of my face. Her wings moved so fast, they seemed to vanish in a blur of light.

She leaned forward and kissed the tip of my nose.

The spot tingled pleasantly, and I was filled with soothing warmth. With another bright wind chime sound, the pixie flitted away and settled back on the butterfly, taking to the air again.

The rest soon followed, meandering higher until the butterfly cloud gathered as one and veered away, back across the field.

"You are blessed, brother," Taeral said with a smile. "A pixie's kiss brings good fortune and long life."

I figured it was blessing enough, just seeing them. It was a moment I'd never forget.

CHAPTER 40

Daoin reappeared in the same place he'd vanished, only without Levoran.

Taeral stood and went to him right away. The rest of us took our time getting up by unspoken consent, giving them a few moments while they embraced without words.

Though he'd lived with us for the past few months, it'd been a long time since Taeral had actually seen his father.

Eventually they came over to the group. Looking at Daoin was disconcerting—I'd only known him as the frail, white-haired version who loved action movies and chocolate milk, and sometimes forgot his own name. This powerful warrior was a stranger to me.

And he was wearing my pendant. I couldn't help thinking of it that way, since I hadn't taken it off once for almost twelve years straight.

Would've been nice to know it was really a sword capable of crippling Fae royalty.

"So." Daoin stopped in front of me. "My son is the DeathSpeaker."

"Seems that way," I said, trying not to sound awkward. Technically, I'd met my father for the first time in my life tonight. And like my brother, the first thing he did was try to kill me.

I hoped I didn't have any more unknown relatives out there. I was going to end up with a serious complex.

"Well, I've waited long enough for this," Daoin said with a grin.

And he pulled me into an embrace.

I hugged him back, thinking how strange it was that this *didn't* feel strange. Because it sure as hell should've. I barely knew this Daoin, and from the little I'd seen, he didn't seem like a hugger. But I felt…accepted.

I felt like family.

He stepped back, and his expression sobered. "Thank you, for what you did for Levoran," he said. "For all of us. It took great courage for you and your lady friend, and Uriskel, to come to Arcadia."

I gave a wry smile. "Well, it took being stubborn and kind of stupid, at least on my part," I said. "I don't know about the rest of them."

"Stubborn," Sadie said. "Definitely stubborn."

"Speak for yourself. I'd only come along to make sure the two of you did not rush headlong into death." Uriskel smiled briefly and walked a few feet away. "And on the topic of stubborn brothers, it's time I got back to mine before he worries himself into doing something foolish," he said. "Shall we cross the Veil?"

Sadie and Reun murmured emphatic agreement and headed after him.

"Come, Father," Taeral said. "The others will be pleased to see you've recovered. Well, at least some of them," he added, shaking his head. "Perhaps not Denei."

"Taeral…" Daoin looked pained. "I cannot return to the human realm."

He froze. "What?"

"Not yet, at least," Daoin said quickly. "I've not recovered completely. There are still… gaps in my mind, blank spaces that must be filled. And only the magic of Arcadia can accomplish that." He looked briefly to the sky. "There are also a few things I must attend to, while I'm here. Some unfinished business."

Taeral's eyes narrowed. "Not with Moirehna."

221

"Gods, no," he said. "Promise or no, I'll not set foot in her palace again." He reached out and clasped Taeral's shoulder. "I will return, as soon as I can. It should not take long."

After a long pause, Taeral said, "I understand, Father."

"Thank you." He smiled sadly, and then faced me and reached for the pendant. "I'll give this back to you now, Gideon," he said.

I waved him off. "No, don't. It belongs to you," I said.

He frowned. "Are you certain?"

"Yeah. I'm pretty sure I can't turn it into a sword," I said. "Besides, if you're going to stay in Arcadia, you'll need it more than me—and I've kind of got the hang of this magic stuff now."

"Magic...stuff." With a bemused smile, Daoin lowered his hand. "All right, then," he said. "I thank you for keeping it safe for me all these years."

"No problem."

There was something else I had to say, and I didn't want to. Just thinking about it left me cold. But it was the right thing—because after everything my brother had been through, he deserved to have what he wanted for once. "Taeral," I said. "You could stay here, too."

His brow furrowed. "Excuse me?"

"In Arcadia. This is your home," I said. "I know you hate the human realm, and you haven't been able to spend time with Daoin in forever. You just got him back." I tried not to think about how much it would suck, not having Taeral around, and went on. "Your promise is pardoned, so there's nothing to stop you from staying here."

"Isn't there?" Taeral quirked a grin. "Brother, you are truly mad if you believe I'll abandon you now," he said. "If I'm not mistaken, we've still a cult to defeat, and a world of Others to save. And there is no one in any realm I'd rather stand beside."

I told myself the tears that pricked my eyes were pure relief. "Same here," I said roughly.

"Well, it seems I've no cause to worry about my sons," Daoin said, beaming his familiar, sunny smile. "You've each other, and that is more than most have."

Right then, I knew it would always be enough.

———————◗◉◖———————

We came through the Veil right where we started—in the middle of Cobalt's living room.

The place was darkened and quiet. Soft light shone beneath a door that I thought was Cobalt and Will's bedroom, but I couldn't remember for sure. It felt like we'd been gone for a year. And the magic of Arcadia was already fading—things here seemed drab and distant, like there was a layer of cotton between me and the world.

I figured I'd get used to it again. But I would miss the intensity of the Fae realm.

Sadie stretched her arms over her head and glanced around. "What time is it, anyway?" she said. "Guess I stopped caring about that over there."

"Late," Uriskel said. "I would guess perhaps two or three in the morning. And Cobalt should be—"

The faintly lit door burst open, and Cobalt charged out like a bear roused from hibernation.

"Right there," Uriskel said with a smirk.

It was all he got out before Cobalt embraced him so hard, he almost knocked them both over. "Do not *ever* do that to me again," he nearly growled. "You hear me? Try it, and I'll banish you from Arcadia myself."

"Good to see you too, brother," Uriskel said in muffled tones. "Perhaps you'd permit me to breathe now."

Cobalt relented and stepped back, swiping his eyes. "Yes, I know," he said. "I'm a great, softhearted dolt."

"I'll forgive you this time."

I knew where he was coming from, but Cobalt seemed a lot more worried than he should've been. And suddenly, I suspected why. "Um...how long were we gone?" I said.

"Ten days." Cobalt's jaw clenched. "Much longer, and I'd have come after you."

I shivered slightly. "Ten *days?*" I said. "How? I mean, it was like two nights there."

"Time is slower in the Fae realm," Uriskel said. "If it moved as quickly as here, we'd all go mad. We live for centuries, after all."

"Aye. Those of us who don't get our stubborn selves killed, at least." With a shudder of relief, Cobalt faced the rest of us. "Thank you for bringing him back in once piece," he said. "It seems you've accomplished your mission. I'm pleased to see you again, Taeral. And this is...your father?" he said, looking at Reun.

Taeral almost laughed. "Daoin elected to stay in Arcadia for a time, as he's unfinished business there. This is our friend, Reun," he said. "Just as great a fool as the rest, as he'd rushed off to rescue us alone."

Reun bowed his head in greeting. "It's true, I'm afraid," he said. "But in the future, I will attempt to consider my actions more carefully."

"A wise idea, that certain brothers of mine should heed."

"Certain brothers?" Uriskel said. "Well, then, you must include Braelan in that. He's leapt first, and looked after, far more often than I."

"I'll blame Braelan later." Cobalt folded his arms and smiled. "Sadie, and Gideon," he said. "I trust you've found what you sought in Arcadia."

"And then some," Sadie said. "But I'm glad to be back."

"Yeah. It was...something else, over there." I shrugged and looked at the floor for a minute. "If you could thank Shade for me, though," I said. "Tell her she was right. Nyantha knew exactly what I needed."

"I will. She'll be glad to hear it," he said.

Uriskel let out a heavy breath. "Well, now that you're sorted, I've a need to get home and let Trystan kill me for leaving him," he said. "Believe it or not…it's good to know all of you. I hope we'll meet again."

"I'm sure we will," I said. "All of you are welcome at the Castle, any time."

"And the Grotto welcomes you," Cobalt said.

"Thanks. We'd better get going, too. Abe probably thinks I'm dead by now, and I'm pretty sure Reun has a death sentence of his own back home."

"Aye, and I'll gladly take her fury," he said. "She'll forgive me. Eventually."

Sadie gave him a look. "I'm not so sure about that. You didn't see how pissed she was."

Reun coughed into his hand. "Well. Perhaps we could stop on the way and purchase flowers? Or some kind of weapon to defend myself with…perhaps a tank."

I had a feeling even that wouldn't be enough. Nuclear was too generous to describe Denei's level of rage.

But I wouldn't mention that.

"I don't know about you guys, but I've had enough portals for a while," I said. "And Abe would've moved my van by now. How about we take a cab?"

Everyone got behind that idea.

CHAPTER 41

My van was parked in its usual spot at the Castle.

I had no idea what that meant, but it didn't seem good. If something happened to Abe while I was gone, if he'd taken the information on Milus Dei and gotten hurt or killed, I'd never forgive myself. Damn it, I should've told him two weeks.

I rushed inside first and found Grygg standing behind the front desk. With Denei and Zoba. Denei glared at me and said, "Where is he?"

"Um..."

My pause was long enough for everyone else to come in. And Denei headed straight for them, fists clenched at her sides. "You stupid, lowdown bastard pig," she snarled. "You were going to die. You *went* there to die, on purpose!" She reached Reun and raised a hand, preparing to slap him like she'd done at least once before.

He caught her wrist, pulled her forward and kissed her. Hard.

And she melted against him with a sob.

"*A'stohr,*" he murmured, embracing her gently. "You've every right to be angry, and I've not the words to apologize. They would not be sufficient." He pressed her hand to his chest. "But please know that my heart is yours—and it will always return to you."

She sniffed and looked up at him. "Well, you'd better find some words right quick, Mister Seelie Noble," she said. "Words that sound like 'I'll never leave you again.'"

"Those words, I can find," he said with a smile. "But perhaps I should demonstrate instead."

Denei grinned. Without a word, she grabbed his shirt and practically dragged him toward the stairs.

Zoba groaned and trudged after them.

"Well, that was…unexpected," Sadie said.

"Yeah," I said absently. I was still worried about the van, and Abe. "Hey, Grygg," I said. "Did my friend stop by while we were gone?"

Grygg gave a ponderous nod. "He is here."

"He's *what*? Here, like at the Castle?"

"Yes. He has come for three nights," Grygg said. "He sleeps in the parlor."

"Jesus, Abe," I muttered with a relieved smile, and headed that way.

The credits of some movie rolled silently on a new big-screen TV at the back of the room. They must've cleaned up and replaced it while we were gone. I found Abe asleep on the big couch, snoring gently.

I almost didn't want to wake him. But he'd kill me if I didn't.

I touched his shoulder, and he jerked toward consciousness. "Whazzat?" he said, blinking blearily. "Remote's on the table."

"Abe. You were supposed to keep the van."

He came awake instantly and bolted upright. After a wide-eyed pause, he shuddered all over and pushed to his feet. "Yeah, well you're supposed to be dead. So I guess you wouldn't know if I kept your damned van."

"Surprise. I'm not."

This time, I hugged him first. And I didn't let go for a long time.

We stepped away eventually, and Abe shook his head. "One of these days, kid," he said. "I'm telling you, I'd better die first—because it ain't gonna be pretty if you go before me."

"Don't even think about it," I said. "You leave me, and I'll come after your ass."

He smiled. "Think I'll stick around for a while. But since you're back from the dead, I'll do it in my own bed tonight." He gave me a firm, one-armed hug and a nod. "Give me a call in the morning, so I can make sure I wasn't dreaming this."

"You got it," I said. "Thanks for not giving up on me."

"Never."

I walked Abe to the door, and he handed me my keys before he left. Then I turned to Taeral and Sadie, who'd waited for me in the lobby. "Is it bedtime now?" I said.

Sadie laughed. "Oh, yeah. I can't wait to sleep on something that's off the ground."

"Aye," Taeral said. "If there's one thing I appreciate in the human realm, it is a proper bed."

"Is that all?" Sadie asked.

"No. I can think of many more things to appreciate," he said huskily.

"Okay. Category of things I don't want to think about." I managed a grin. For some reason, I wasn't as jealous as I would've been before—I was kind of happy for them, and hoped they'd be able to have something more than the sort-of relationship that wasn't enough for either of them. Even if they were both too stubborn to admit it. "Listen, I'm probably going to take a quick nap, but there's something I have to do before I hit the hay too hard," I said. "So don't worry if I'm not here. I won't be gone long."

Taeral frowned. "What is it? If you need help, I'll—"

"No. I have to do this on my own," I said. "It's not dangerous. I promise."

"All right. If you're certain..."

I waved a hand at them. "Go on. Honestly, I'm fine."

They walked toward the stairs, and I waited until they were out of sight to slip through the door. I'd grab a nap in my van, for old time's sake. But not because I had to.

Being home would never scare me again.

I wore my best suit for the occasion.

Okay, it was my only suit. But I felt pretty good in the clothes the mirror mender made for me—like I was something more than what I'd believed myself to be most of my life. Worthless, pointless, human waste who didn't matter to anyone. Someone who could drop dead at any time, and not one thing in the world would change.

That wasn't me anymore. I knew what family meant now, and I had one of my own. One I truly belonged to.

That was what this trip was about.

I parked the van by the open gates and went in. It was late enough, or early enough, to have the place to myself. By now I had no problem finding the right spot, and I walked there slowly, my mind whirling with anticipation...and maybe a little concern.

Would she know me? What would she think of me now?

I slowed even more as my destination came into view. I had to force myself the last few steps, and then I sat cross-legged on the ground, just staring at the inscription.

JESSAMYN ROSE HADLEY

"All right," I murmured aloud. "Stop stalling."

I closed my eyes and reached down without moving. Felt the sensation of cool earth, then polished wood, rotting material, and finally bone. The unseen rubber band snapped back. My head throbbed, and I focused on the gravestone in front of me until it shifted and became a woman.

She was just as beautiful as I'd imagined.

My throat seized, and I couldn't say a word. Her face was so smooth, so pure. And her smile was everything.

"Gideon. Oh, my sweet boy. I never imagined I'd be able to see you."

I smiled as a warm tear tracked down my face. And I finally found my voice.

"Hello…Mom."

Thanks for reading!

If you enjoyed REALM OF MIRRORS, please consider leaving a review on Amazon to share your thoughts. Reviews are a great way to help other readers find new books and new authors to enjoy.

You can also visit my Amazon author page and follow me on Amazon to be among the first notified when RETURN OF THE HUNTERS, book four of The DeathSpeaker Codex, is released.

About the Author

Sonya Bateman lives in "scenic" Central New York, with its two glorious seasons: winter and road construction. She is the author of the Gavyn Donatti urban fantasy series (Master of None / Master and Apprentice) from Simon & Schuster. Under the pseudonym S.W. Vaughn, she's the author of the Skin Deep paranormal M/M erotic romance series (Loose Id) and the House Phoenix thriller series.

You can contact her at sonyabateman.author@gmail.com.

CPSIA information can be obtained at www.ICGtesting.com
Printed in the USA
LVOW11s2321231016

509976LV00001B/67/P

9 781532 946868